Barlow Comes to Judgement

A body buried on the moors: a photograph muti-
lated so that its subjects cannot be identified.
Barlow discovers the body on his original northern
patch; he gets possession of the photograph after
an encounter in an East End pub. Establishing
the link takes him to Soho, to Cyprus, and to the
very seat of justice in England.

The pressures upon him – both criminal and
awesomely official – would crack a milder man,
but his determination increases as the obstacles
get more formidable. His triumph, though, is not
sweet.

By the same author
Barlow in Charge

Barlow Comes to Judgement

Elwyn Jones

Arthur Barker Limited London

FOR JOHN LLOYD, friend and
colleague.

*The character of Detective Chief Inspector Barlow was created
for the original Z Cars series by Troy Kennedy Martin. This
novel is published by arrangement with him and with the BBC
and with grateful acknowledgement to Barlow's other 'creator',
Stratford Johns.*

Scenery meant very little to Detective Chief Superintendent Barlow, but this one view always took his breath away. The train slowed as it approached the bridge – and there below, at its widest, at its most sluggishly powerful, lay the Manchester Ship Canal. It was Barlow's frontier. Here the North of England began. From now on he was back home.

He glanced as though for reassurance at the fat OHMS brief-case on the luggage rack, and at his bowler hat beside it. At Preston station he knew a car would be waiting for him – a black Jaguar, an Assistant Chief Constable's car, with an ACC's driver. That was protocol for Mr Barlow of the Home Office. He believed though that for Charlie Barlow, detective or 'jack' as they were still called in the North, there would also be one of his kind to greet him. He hoped there would be.

The train pulled into Warrington – Preston two stops away. Barlow got up and reached for his luggage and his bowler and left the train. The reception committee would be meeting the one o'clock train from Euston. This was the eleven o'clock. He had two hours in hand. It would be time enough.

Quickly he walked through the station and out onto the forecourt. There was one taxi parked fifty yards away. Barlow walked across and leant against the driver's window.

The driver listened to his instructions and then shrugged. 'It's your money. You sitting in the back?'

Barlow got in the front. They hit the motorway quite soon.

'Easier to get around now anyroad,' said Barlow. The driver nodded: 'Folks think nothing of driving twenty, thirty miles for a drink or a night out.'

'Or to commit crime,' thought Barlow, and kept the notion to himself. As miles passed he remembered PC 231 Barlow who had ridden a bicycle along roads a great deal narrower and less well lit than this. It had been 1946 and he had just finished with two years of killing people. He had become a soldier straight from school and the police seemed a sensible choice for a young, strong man who did not know what to do but was used to taking orders. He remembered his first station sergeant reflecting one evening: 'There's only three things in this life. You can work for your money or you can steal – or you can become a copper.'

It had been a toss-up for Barlow. Like so many good 'jacks' his nose for crime could once have sniffed in the opposite direction. He would have made a fairly good villain, thought Barlow. He had all the qualities, including an instinctive distrust of formal rules which only long years of disciplined service had taught him to curb. By now he could have been the proud owner of a splendid house in Cheshire, a flash Mercedes and a corner seat in the local golf club. As it was – he glanced into the back of the car – he had a bowler hat.

'Want to get out?' The car slowed almost to a halt and Barlow gazed up at the span of the bridge – the 'new' bridge that crossed the Mersey at Widnes was high above him.

'No,' he said. 'I just want a shufti.'

The driver shrugged and eased the car forward. Barlow looked back at the round, brick building that marked the site of the old ferry which had winched half a dozen cars across the

river. A slow, tedious journey it had been, too, with the only alternative a round trip of a dozen miles or more. Liverpool had been a foreign city then, remote across the river. Now, as Barlow looked up, he could see cars streaming across high above him. He wound down his window. The place looked cleaner, but the smell of chemicals was still heavy in the air. The people were better dressed but they still had the pallor of those who get their sun filtered. Widnes was still a town in which no birds sang, and there were no moths.

'Enough work around?' The driver nodded: 'Not so bad. The chemicals are still here – ICI, Mond, British Oxygen, Du Pont. Don't pay as much as the car blokes do. There's a lot do a bit of travelling now and go to work for Fords. Can't blame them. It's dirty work at the chemicals, most of it. But there's a lot still stick with the old names. At least they're part of the place.'

So, unchanged, was the 'dock' area. No boats unloaded there now. The basin was a tangled mess of rotting barges, rusty metal drums and stagnant water. Timber was piled around and, beyond, Barlow could see the British Oxygen plant. Faintly on the breeze came the familiar smell of the bonemeal factory. Alongside the road were the grey-red tippings of the chemical works, lying dead like the lava of an extinct volcano. Beyond was another flattened, artificial mountain, but this time the colour was dirty white. His boyhood had been spent among these mounds. Where some children had walked or played in fields he and his friends had scuffed their way across playgrounds of hard-packed chemical waste, emerald, black, russet and olive.

One particular heap, Barlow remembered, would lie around the next corner. It didn't. Instead there was a large traffic roundabout, concrete walling enclosing the central island. There were even strips of grass! Widnes would never become a garden city but at least somebody was trying to clean up the

worst of the past. He looked at his watch and turned to the driver.

'Right. Back to the station. I have a train to get off.'

The passengers arriving at Preston on the one o'clock train from Euston walked up the slope and out into the station yard. Detective Chief Superintendent Barlow was among them. He paused on the pavement and a police driver appeared alongside him.

'Mr Barlow? The car's right here, sir.'

It was, as Barlow had expected, one of the ACC's cars. He looked around for Jim Dawson, once his colleague on a beat in Widnes, now Detective Chief Superintendent of the county force. The familiar figure was nowhere to be seen.

The driver held the door for him.

Barlow kept any expression off his face. But as if reading his thoughts, the driver said: 'Mr Dawson sent his apologies, sir. He's a bit tied up but he said he hoped to be free when you got to HQ.'

Barlow nodded acknowledgement. A message from Chief Superintendent Dawson to Mr Barlow from the Home Office. So be it. He jammed his bowler more firmly on his head.

As the car swept into the barrack-square-like forecourt of police headquarters Barlow grinned at the driver. 'Stop here, lad. I want to walk up to the door . . . Don't look so bothered. I just want to do a small security check. Thanks for the drive.'

He got out and strolled casually up the steps without even a glance at the television camera he knew scanned the door. There was no one at the desk. Barlow waited, then let out one loud shout: 'Shop!'

'Afternoon sir.'

Barlow looked at him. 'Bert Prendergast. Started service in Kirby.'

For a second there was a gratified grin on the sergeant's face. Then it froze again and the shoulders pulled themselves back into line.

'Yes, sir. Mr Dawson told me to show you straight in.'

Barlow followed him in silence. As they marched along a young policeman clutching a file of papers flattened himself against the wall, respect for rank oozing stiffly out of him. Barlow repressed a sudden urge to kick him. The sergeant opened a door and stood aside.

'Mr Barlow, sir.'

There were three men in the room. Chief Superintendent Jim Dawson came around from behind his desk, his hand outstretched.

'Welcome to the industrial north.'

There were two other men in the room and Barlow knew them – Arthur Bolt and Ken Wilson, both with CID experience, but now Chief Superintendents in charge of two of the county's largest divisions. They exchanged nods. Dawson moved towards a drinks cabinet that was already open.

'Too early in the day for you?'

Barlow looked around at the three of them. 'Was it ever?'

The glass of Scotch he was handed was full to the brim. Even had he wanted water or soda there wouldn't have been room. Barlow suppressed a grin.

'And how is the decadent south?'

It was Arthur Bolt who asked the question. He was slumped in his seat, large, regular teeth bared in a grin that wouldn't have looked out of place on an Alsatian. Barlow lifted his glass.

'Warmer than this place.'

'And how's everything in Whitehall?'

This time it was Ken Wilson, square-faced, snub-nosed, with an expression like a large worried baby. He had broken up the county's only symptoms of gang warfare by demonstrat-

ing forcefully and rapidly that he was rougher than anyone the gangs could find to lead them.

'My in-tray is full. How's yours?'

Wilson shrugged and got up to pour himself another drink.

'You know me. I prefer pushing people around.'

Barlow let that one pass. It was too early. Instead, he turned to Jim Dawson.

'You caught that feller yet?'

There was no need to ask which 'feller'. The county force had been searching all week for one of their local villains, a man with a record of violence, who had escaped from Durham jail.

'Not yet. We will though. He's too thick to stay out more than a fortnight.'

'Remember the first time we picked him up?'

Arthur Bolt had a far away gleam in his eye.

'My first case as DS. Stolen wallpaper it was. We got a tip-off that he was the one who'd nicked it. He was living next door to his mother then. I called at his mother's, showed her my warrant card and said to her: "I believe you have some stolen wallpaper?" She just opened the door wide and said: "That's right, love. It's all laid out upstairs". When I arrested her she said: "Oh dear, I thought you'd come to buy some". Then we went next door. His wife answered the door and said he was ill in bed. I went up to talk to him, and there he is lying groaning and pretending he's got 'flu. I looked at him and I thought there was something odd about him. Then I worked it out. His left leg was on one side, his right leg was on the other and he had a third leg down the middle. So I yanked the bed-clothes off him – and there are six rolls of wallpaper between his knees. He just looked at me and said: "How did you know they were there?"'

The talk drifted, desultory and fairly aimless. Barlow's glass

was refilled promptly whenever the level sank more than half an inch. He had sat through many such occasions in rooms like this. But now most of the names were new to him. The ones he knew had been promoted or sent to gaol. The other three were using the elliptical shorthand of close colleagues talking shop. Barlow was a stranger – and his status was being underlined.

Abruptly he got to his feet.

'Mind if I take a look at your control room, Jim?'

Dawson had been pouring a drink. His hand stopped over the glass. He gave Barlow a look that was half suspicion, half challenge.

'Be my guest. They call it the Operations Room now.'

He crossed to a phone and picked it up. Within two minutes a young uniformed inspector appeared in the room and surveyed the assembled group with a carefully neutral expression. Jim waved a hand towards him.

'Inspector Pearson ... Mr Barlow from the Home Office. He would like to watch your band of performing seals up there.'

'Certainly, sir.'

The Inspector opened the door and turned to Barlow. 'If you would care to follow me, sir, I'll lead the way.'

The long room they walked into looked like a telephone exchange with half a dozen television sets standing about in the middle of it. The Inspector took up his stance behind a raised desk at the far end. He launched into what was obviously his set-piece, stressing the fact that each man was responsible only for a specific area but had overall control of vehicles in that area. Barlow suddenly realised that young Inspector Pearson thought he was talking to a civil servant – and a civilian. He was tempted to disabuse him sharply, but he restrained himself. It wasn't the Inspector he was at odds with, it was Jim Dawson.

The Inspector was explaining that the three girls at the far end of the room took all motorway breakdown calls, which in this area always came to the police first. Barlow remembered when that decision had been taken by the then Chief Constable and all the grumbling it had caused about 'Who does he think we are – the AA?'

The Inspector moved into part two of his patter and started flicking switches on his desk to demonstrate how he could eavesdrop on any and every channel. He punched up the closed circuit television cameras that monitored the building, and Barlow started to look duly impressed, then decided he was bored with the masquerade.

'Why wasn't I stopped?'

'I beg your pardon, sir?'

'Why wasn't I stopped? I entered this building a couple of hours ago. I entered alone since the driver was parking his car. I am not known here. Why wasn't I stopped?'

'But we were expecting you, sir.'

'You were expecting a Mr Barlow from the Home Office. How did you know he was me?'

'Because you looked like ...' The Inspector broke off sheepishly. His eyes had unconsciously strayed to the top of Barlow's head.

'Because I had bowler hat on. . . ? What makes you think that some smart lad from the Provisionals isn't capable of buying one and wearing it?'

The Inspector came to a sensible decision. He straightened up, looked Barlow firmly in the face and said: 'Sorry, sir. It won't happen again.'

Barlow felt better. He nodded at the television sets in the middle of the floor.

'Those are new. What do they do?'

His guide's eyes had flickered slightly at the 'new' but he

seized on the distraction gratefully.

'I'll show you, sir.'

He led the way towards the nearest set, knelt in front of it and flicked a switch. A street map of Preston appeared. He swivelled a knob and the map slid across the screen.

'We're rather proud of these, sir. They were developed here. We can use them for monitoring any mobile operation.'

He turned another knob and the map swung immediately into larger scale. Another turn of the knob and the scale became larger still until a square mile was filling the screen with every side-road and alleyway shown in detail. Barlow was impressed and said so. With the score evened he left the control room, refusing an escort back to Jim Dawson's office. Behind the now closed door the Inspector took a few deep breaths. Along the length of the room the men at the desks kept their heads down and looked even busier than they were. None of them had actually been eavesdropping, but as police-men they were sensitive to atmosphere and they all knew that within the next five minutes someone was going to get it in the neck.

When Barlow got back to the office, Bolt and Wilson had gone. Dawson was behind his desk, his tie loosened but with nothing else to indicate that he had a great deal of whisky resting in his stomach. He looked up as Barlow came in and nodded towards the empty chairs.

'They had to be off – asked me to say cheerio.'

Barlow nodded an acknowledgement and crossed to the window. Behind him there was a faint scratching as Jim Dawson scrawled his name on various letters and notices. Barlow waited until the 'signing up' was over.

'Got your car here?'

'Yes.'

'If we can get out of this place I'll buy you a drink.'

There was a silence while the two of them exchanged level glances. Then Jim nodded.

'Alright. Let's go.'

They were in the car before they spoke again.

'Where do you want to aim for?'

Barlow settled himself back in his seat. 'Let's go to Widnes.'

If Jim Dawson saw anything unusual in being asked to drive twenty miles when there were perfectly good pubs within a few hundred yards he gave no sign of it. He merely nodded an acknowledgement. His radio was giving out the steady bleeping noise which meant the channel was engaged. When the bleeps ended he picked up his phone and gave his 'Headquarters Eight' call-sign and got an immediate answer.

'I'm going to Widnes.'

The information was acknowledged. It would also be passed on: within a few minutes the men of that division would know that the Head of CID was on his way to their patch. The radio was turned low, but Barlow knew that Dawson would always hear his own call sign: it was a knack they all acquired. Dawson eventually broke the silence: 'We can't go to "The Coachman". They've pulled it down.'

'Yes,' said Barlow. 'I know.'

Dawson glanced at him, but did not give Barlow the satisfaction of asking how he knew. Eventually they left the motorway and swung down the long main shopping street. Jim Dawson drove on and turned the car into one of the suburbs of Hough Green. At one time it had been the height of Barlow's ambition to own a house here. The one he had particularly wanted – it had bay windows – was still there on the left. On the right, however, there were new housing estates and new roads. The car turned down one of them and pulled up outside a low redbrick pub.

They went inside. It was spacious, with tables and chairs

and carpet underfoot. The lighting was soft and there was an elaborate buffet bar set out in the corner with an array of cheeses and cold meats. Along one wall was a huge, sprawling mural of a bandy-legged shepherd staring in a puzzled way at half a dozen knock-kneed sheep. Barlow remembered that the place was called 'The Good Shepherd'.

He strode to the bar and ordered two large scotches. He downed his in one swallow.

'Right,' he said. 'Let's go.'

'Go where?'

'Let's go to a pub,' said Barlow as he turned and headed for the door.

He stood beside the car as Jim Dawson joined him. Jim got in, reached across and unlocked the door on Barlow's side. Barlow got in and settled himself comfortably. Jim sat staring straight ahead, his hand resting on the wheel. 'Where to?'

'Let's go to the "Station Arms",' said Barlow.

'There's a new one-way system. I'm not sure I know the best way there.'

'That's alright,' said Barlow comfortingly. 'I do.'

Ten minutes later they drew up outside the 'Station Arms'. It had been one of Barlow's favourites. A large pub with half a dozen small bars, all bearing different and faintly baffling titles – Smoke Room, Snug, Private, Saloon – and all with precisely the same shabby furniture and dark yellow wallpaper. The main bar, he remembered, had a long row of cubicles formed by high-backed benches. It had been a favourite of couples on their way to or from the dances at the YMCA opposite.

He pushed his way impatiently through the doors, and the sound of the juke box hit him hard over the head. The cubicles had gone. Instead there was a vast open space of bare floor flanked by three fruit machines and the juke box. It wasn't a pub any more, it was a large drinking barn. He turned his head

and caught Jim Dawson's sardonic eye. For a second he was tempted to head for the railway station in a rage; turn away from this place, these people, and never come back. Instead he took Jim Dawson firmly by the arm and led him towards the bar. They sat on stools alongside each other and Barlow suddenly grinned: 'What you having? My name's Charlie Barlow. I used to drink here.'

'I know,' said Jim slowly. 'I once had to come in here and get you out. You were on the floor trying to make an arrest with the feller you were after on top beating lumps out of you. I'll have a Scotch and if you try and knock anybody off tonight – you're on your own.'

Two hours later Detective Chief Superintendent Charles Barlow was aware that he had drink taken. A stranger would have found it difficult to tell, but one or two close acquaintances, plus a couple of criminals, would have noticed a faint glitter in the eyes and made a note to tread carefully. He and Jim had progressed through four pubs and about fifteen years of past history. They had now got to the point in Jim's career where he had been 'borrowed' from the police force for six months in order to investigate racecourse security. In the course of his investigation he became the only policeman investigating racecourse security to get himself thrown off a racecourse. He also caused some consternation by informing the aristocratic gentlemen then in charge of racing that there was little point in conducting elaborate dope tests for drugs when everyone except them knew that the best way to 'gee up' a horse was to feed it half a bottle of whisky.

'Did I ever tell you the story about the bent trainer and the Duke of Norfolk?' Jim told stories well. Barlow settled down to listen . . .

'You know what I mean by "balling" a horse – giving it dope in a ball of sugar?'

Barlow nodded.

'Right. The scene is Ascot. The Duke is parading about the paddock when he sees this trainer who's a bit dodgy, and the trainer is feeding sugar balls to his horse. So the Duke lets out a great yell: "You there. Over here".

'The trainer trots over to the Duke, who says: "Were you balling that horse?"

' "Good Heavens no, your Grace."

'The Duke looks a bit dubious. Then he says: "Alright. Off you go".

'The trainer starts back to the horse when the Duke lets out another shout: "Come back here".

'Back comes the trainer. His Grace fixes him with a steely glare and says: "Do you have any more of those sugar balls?"

' "Well, as a matter of fact, your Grace, yes I do."

' "Would you be prepared to eat one?"

'The trainer turns a bit pale but he looks the Duke straight in the eye, takes a sugar ball out of his pocket and swallows it. The Duke stares at him for a bit and then says: "Would you be prepared to see me eat one?"

' "Certainly, your Grace."

'Whereupon he hands the Duke a sugar ball, the Duke gulps it down, coughs a couple of times and then says, grudgingly: "Alright. Off you go".

'Off the trainer does go. When he gets to the horse, the jockey says: "What was all that about?"

"Never you mind," says the trainer. "You just ride the race. But if anybody passes you in the straight, don't worry – it will be either me or the Duke of Norfolk".'

With his usual impeccable timing, Dawson turned away on

the last line and walked across to the bar. Barlow followed him and together they leant on the stained, scarred counter looking through into the public bar opposite. The shabby bare room was lit by two bare bulbs. Sitting on the benches along the wall were ten men all dressed in the same uniform of greasy caps, flannel shirts unbuttoned at the neck and shabby, torn jackets. Nine of them had previous. The tenth had a clean record, though, according to Jim Dawson, one of his detective sergeants planned to remedy that in the very near future. One youngish man's face looked vaguely familiar. Barlow nodded towards him: 'What's his name?'

Jim told him and Barlow felt depressed. He knew why the face was familiar: he had once arrested his father. He picked up his glass.

'I feel old.'

'You are old,' said Dawson with brutal cheerfulness. 'We both are, Charlie. Old men in a dry month waiting for crime statistics while younger men go out and chase the baddies for us. But at least I come down and inspect the place occasionally. All you ever see are the insides of files. Still, I suppose somebody has to do it and I'd rather it was a Lancashire lad than some softy from the South.'

Barlow groaned to himself. He had hoped that that particular line of attack had been abandoned two hours ago.

'I've met one or two softies from the South who would eat you for breakfast, Jim. And wash you down with gin and tonic afterwards.'

'Speaking of which . . .' Dawson pushed himself away from the bar. 'Do you want to stay in this squalor any longer recapturing the days of your youth? Personally, I've developed a strong liking for plush lounge bars in comfortable hotels. The chairs are more comfortable and you meet a better class of

criminal. Anyway,' he raised his voice to include the landlord, 'it's way after closing time and we're giving this villain an excuse to break the law.'

Barlow looked around him. All those years ago, when he had been a brand-new constable in a brand-new helmet walking nervously around, this had been the rag-totters' pub. This was where you came in search of information about lead from church roofs, lengths of copper piping from factory yards. The lad sitting in the corner whose face had looked familiar – Barlow remembered the night his father had gone out to a row of back-to-back houses, taking his hacksaw with him. Patiently and steadily he had started to saw off the two inches of lead overflow pipe that stuck out of the wall on forty-two outside lavatories. He had been on his thirty-ninth when PC Barlow came round the corner. The two of them had known each other for years but that had not stopped him trying to brain Barlow with the bagful of lead and it had not stopped Barlow bringing him in. The encounter had cost Barlow a nasty headache; his opponent had ended up with the then traditional sentence: six months for every hundredweight.

Outside they both took a deep breath and Barlow asked cautiously:

'You fit?'

Dawson was in the driving seat before he replied:

'Steady as a rock. Anyway, even the traffic bobbies know the number of this car.'

He headed back towards the hotel in which Barlow was booked. With his left hand he automatically reached down and clicked the radio on. They heard a message about an accident on the motorway. Then, as the car swung round behind the market, they heard a message to all mobiles in their area . . .

'Intruders on premises of British Oxygen disturbed by security man. Intruders have made off in the direction of the bridge. Three men . . .'

The information continued but Barlow suddenly sat up and spoke over them.

'Next on the left.'

Instinctively, Dawson obeyed the instruction. Then he turned and looked at Barlow.

'What's the idea?'

Barlow nodded towards the radio.

'We're mobile. We're in the area. In fact, we're probably the nearest.'

'We're old men, Charlie. Remember? We sit in offices nowadays. It's the youngsters go dashing about in the dark after tearaways.'

The car took another corner and started heading into the 'dock' area. It looked even more desolate in the headlights than it had on Barlow's visit that morning. Barlow sat up and peered into the darkness.

'That's alright, Jim. You can stay in the car.'

There was no reply. Instead the car accelerated. Dawson reached down, picked up his hand-set and snapped out his call-sign. It was acknowledged immediately. But when he spoke it was casually and informally.

'We're in the dock area. Myself and Mr Barlow. Tell your lads not to jump us by mistake.'

He dropped the receiver back in its rest and swung the car down a side alleyway.

'They won't thank us for poking our noses in . . . Where is that damn factory anyway?'

'Down there,' said Barlow pointing. 'They were heading for the bridge. If we stopped behind that factory we should cut them off.'

Dawson raised an eyebrow at him. 'A good memory for local geography?'

The question hung in the air. Barlow didn't enlighten him. Instead, he pointed. Ahead of them was a running figure. Dawson grabbed for his phone and spoke quickly and urgently. With his other hand, he skidded the car around a corner as the man ducked and dodged to try and escape the beam that was pinning him. Suddenly he vanished. Dawson swore.

'He's in the lard factory.'

As the car rocked to a halt, Barlow grabbed the torch from the dashboard in front of him, threw open his door and scrambled out. As he ran forward he heard Dawson shout but no words reached him. He shouldered past the corner of a building, skidded and almost fell. The wooden boards beneath his feet were greasy and slimy. There was a stink of rancid fat in his nostrils. He remembered from the morning seeing the huge black boilers with globules of white fat spilling from them and lumps of it lying about the catwalks. It had put him off lard at the time; now it made him choke and he could taste the whisky in his throat.

Ahead of him a door stood half open. There was no sign of the man who had opened it. Nightwatchman perhaps? But if so, where was he? He remembered seeing a sign, 'Guard dogs operate', and a wooden watchtower. Presumably, the dogs and their owner were after the intruder. He heard some distance away a faint barking and a shout. Slowly he moved forward, flicking his torch on and off into the darker corners. The torch picked up a gleam of eyes and a rat scurried past Barlow's feet. He switched the torch off as he came to the side of the building. For a few sconds he stood still. Then carefully he moved forward. With one hand outstretched he felt his way around. His hand touched cloth and something hit him hard across the

side of the head. As he fell he heard in his head through the bright light Jim Dawson's voice . . . 'Old men in a dry month.' He tensed for a boot to crash at his ribs but there was nothing – just the thick film of grease under his face.

'Here he is. Lift him . . . gently now.'

It was Jim Dawson's voice coming from a long way away. Then there were hands under his arm-pits and he was heaved to his feet.

'Are you alright, sir?'

It was a young voice and an anxious one. Barlow guessed its owner wasn't accustomed to hauling Chief Supers to their feet. He shook his head. It hurt but the mist cleared a little.

'Did you get him?'

He heard Jim Dawson's chuckle.

'He's alright . . . Yes, Charlie, they did. If it's any consolation he was in such a hurry after clocking you that he ran straight into a patrol car. We've never had such an efficient ferret.'

Barlow winced – and not entirely from pain. The mockery left Dawson's voice.

'Come on, lad – a doctor for you.'

'No,' said Barlow, straightening up. 'I don't need one. I need a brandy – a large one – balm for injured pride.'

'Are you sure? . . . Alright. Three-star balm coming up.' There was a pause and the gently mocking note crept back into the voice. 'Do you want him charged?'

'No.' It was short and explosive like a pistol shot.

'Right.' Dawson turned away and then tossed his instructions to one of the car crew. 'Throw in offensive weapon though. And pile it on. After all,' he said, tucking a hand in Barlow's arm, 'We can't have the baddies thinking they can slug Chief Supers and get away with it.'

They drove back to the hotel in silence. A night porter came

to answer their ring. His look of instant antagonism as he caught sight of Barlow changed to relief as Jim Dawson appeared behind him.

'Good evening, Mr Dawson. Is this you. . . . ?' His voice tailed away.

'Yes, Percy. Mr Barlow had a slight mishap in the course of duty so that other villains like you can sleep soundly in their beds . . . Give me your coat, Charlie.'

Barlow looked down at himself and realised he was heavily smeared in mud, slime and white streaks of lard. Dawson handed the overcoat to the porter.

'See if you can do something with that, Percy.'

Percy was visibly appalled, but sensible night porters try to oblige senior policemen.

'And bring us a couple of large brandies.'

He led the way into the lounge and gently pushed Barlow down into an armchair.

'Let's have a look at that head.'

His fingers probed above Barlow's left ear.

'No, you're alright. It was a hard but flat – a piece of four by two, I should think. Nothing broken . . . Thank you, Percy. We'll look after ourselves.'

The porter pocketed a coin and went away. Barlow took a swallow of brandy and felt better. He looked across at Dawson.

'I take it you had more sense than to come after me.'

'You take it correctly, Charlie. I got on the radio and told control you were in there. I said they were to tell the boys to tell the dogs not to bite anything wearing a bowler hat.'

Barlow got to his feet. He had had more than enough for one evening. He looked down at Jim Dawson. 'I'll see you at nine.'

Dawson looked startled. 'You still want to go? That early, I mean.'

'It's what I came for.'

'Why don't you sleep it off for a bit? I'll call them and tell them to hold it until after lunch.'

'Nine o'clock.'

'Alright.'

Dawson shrugged and moved towards the swing doors.

'On your head be it,' and with a wave of the hand he left. Barlow turned on his heel, picked up his case and headed for the stairs. When he reached his room he dumped the case on the bed and looked at his watch. It said two o'clock.

At eight-thirty Chief Superintendent Barlow was ploughing through bacon, sausage, tomato, black pudding and aspirin. He was staring grimly at the *Daily Telegraph* and willing his headache to go away. Slowly and painfully, his headache was responding. By the time Dawson arrived it had reduced itself to a dull steady throbbing, centred mainly around a large lump above his ear. Jim tactfully refrained from asking Barlow how he felt. 'It's all laid on. They'll be waiting for us.'

They drove for a few miles and then turned off a dual carriageway onto a surprisingly rural road surrounded by fields and farm buildings. The explanation emerged a hundred yards further on with a sign announcing the presence of an agricultural college. They swung off the road and drove towards a low red building with a series of grey concrete huts behind. As they got out a sergeant wearing wellingtons strolled across to them.

Dawson performed introductions: 'Harry Hastings, Mr Barlow . . . Harry's the king of the County's dogs.'

As they turned the corner a double line of concrete kennels with strong wire fronts stretched ahead of them. Some forty Alsatians began to bark and Barlow's head began to ache again. Grimly he ploughed on. As they passed each cage, the police

sergeant pushed a hand through and pulled an ear or ruffled a head. According to temperament the dogs stood with eager paws on the wire or, the more nervous ones these, whirled around and around in their cages in a frenzy of excitement. Finally, as the hammers in Barlow's head beat harder and harder, they came to the last cage in the line. The Sergeant stood in front of it.

'There she is. That's Meg.'

In the cage a small sheepdog stood quietly, showing no sign of excitement at all. Her ears were flattened along her head, her tail was down. She had the slightly cowed look that all good working sheepdogs have. Her eyes were fixed on the Sergeant.

'She doesn't look much, does she?'

It was Dawson who made the comment. Jim liked his dogs to be as extrovert and robust as he was.

'She may not look much but she can do it. We've tried her eight times now on the full test. And she's done it every time. No bother at all.'

'Is she the only one?'

It was Barlow's question. The Sergeant puffed his pipe before answering.

'No. We've got Rex. He's an Alsatian. He's one of my two. But I've got him at home at the moment. He's got a bit nervous recently, jumping at everything ... noises, even car headlights. So I've taken him off work.'

'But this one's alright?'

'Yes.'

Barlow turned to Dawson. 'Let's get on with it.'

The Sergeant opened the door and slipped a leash on the sheepdog. They walked back down the row of cages to the full chorus of dogs. Spots danced in front of Barlow's eyes but he stared grimly ahead and eventually the noise died away. They

reached a field behind the yard and the Sergeant opened a gate.

'Right. This field is an acre and a half. There's a pig's head buried about fifty yards from that hedge, roughly half way along.'

'How long has it been there?' asked Barlow.

'Eighteen months.'

The Sergeant glanced at Dawson and received a nod. He bent over the dog, unslipped the leash and whispered a command to it several times. The dog began to move across the field with a fast flattened run, its nose to the ground. It completed a long fast curve and then began working its way back. It circled past them, ignoring them completely, and started a second cast. This time it was much nearer the spot where the pig's head was buried. Gradually it began to work its way towards it. Then suddenly it stopped and began tearing at the ground with its paws. The whole search had taken less than five minutes.

The Sergeant ran over to order the dog away. It was now throwing earth up in all directions. Dawson nodded towards it.

'If it was the real thing the handler would have to stay with it.'

Barlow looked a query.

'Because if she finds a body she'll start to eat it. She doesn't know the difference after all.'

The hammering in Barlow's head was joined by a slight surging of the stomach.

'But you reckon she could do it? The real thing?'

The Sergeant was back with them and it was he who answered. 'Yes, sir. She could find a body. How long it would take would depend on what kind of info you could give us. But in the end she'd find it.'

'How long could it have been there?'

'It's a bit hard to say. We haven't really had time to find out. But they found a body over the other side of the county two months back. Some tramp. Natural causes. It had been there six years. I took her over. And when we got to the spot she got excited and started scrabbling around. And the body wasn't even there anymore.'

When they got back to the main building the other dog-handlers had large cups of tea for them. Barlow ladled sugar gratefully into his. He looked around. Behind him the wall was stacked with boxes of infant cereal food. 'What are those for?'

The Sergeant chuckled: 'We get them from the local supermarket. They're all date-stamped so they can't sell them after a certain time. Any left over they pass on to us. Good for growing dogs.'

'If the makers knew they'd have a fit.'

Jim Dawson got to his feet.

'If you've seen enough, Charlie, we'll push off and let these two get on with looking for fleas or whatever they do with themselves during the day.'

They drove back in silence. Barlow was determined not to make the first move. The ball was in Jim's court – and he was leaving it there. As they turned into the sprawling expanse of buildings that was the county headquarters they passed a row of private houses – accommodation for married officers. Dawson reached for his handset: 'Headquarters Eight.'

A keen young voice acknowledged his call-sign immediately.

'I've just come round behind the married quarters. There's a red sports car parked at the back of Number Six. Probably alright . . . Mebbe belongs to somebody visiting. But cars don't normally park there. Check it out, will you? No need to make a fuss. Just make sure it's alright.'

He swung into the car park, glancing half apologetically at Barlow.

'It won't do any harm. And it keeps them on their toes.'

Barlow reached for the door handle.

'I agree with you. A careful copper is a safe one.'

An hour later they were standing in a corner of the head-quarters' club. Barlow was clutching a glass of beer and watching Jim Dawson who was sipping Scotch and taking a long time to come to the point. Gradually the bar behind them filled up. Barlow recognised the Inspector from the Commerce Branch, which was how fair-minded officialdom liked to refer to the Fraud Squad. Two detective sergeants from the Special Branch were relating with a mixture of humour and resignation an account of a forthcoming trial in which a man arrested for IRA activities was due to tell the court how they had tortured him to make him confess. Barlow caught the last sentence: '. . . Then he says we burned him with cigarette ends. A bit unfair 'cos we don't smoke . . .'

Jim suddenly leant forward. About time too thought Barlow. 'You remember the Bunscombe case?'

Barlow did. Jim had been the officer in charge of inquiries into an appalling series of murders. The victims had been young girls in their early teens, young drifters whose disappearances were routinely noted then forgotten. The Bunscombe case was one Dawson seldom talked about, and never in public.

This time he did. 'Remember how we found the second body?' He took a long swig at his drink. 'We had acres of the moorland to search. We had one of the biggest search parties ever – and we could have missed that body. We very nearly did. You know the line had gone past. And a young PC . . . It was his first week in the Force. He dropped back to take a

pump. And when he turned round there was this kid's hand sticking out of the ground right by his feet . . . Well now we've got the dogs. It's taken a long time to train them. But any search for bodies now and those dogs will be out so fast their paws won't touch the ground. You know that. At least, you know it now . . .'

He paused and stared into his glass. Barlow sat not saying a word. Jim looked up suddenly.

'There are three girls still missing, Charlie. At least three, all with some links, some possible links with Bunscombe. When we took him in he just clammed up. I tried all ways and *nothing* would make him talk, nothing He admitted one murder. We proved four others.'

'And there are still three more?'

'In his secret valley.'

'His what?'

'He wouldn't talk but he did write, to his brother mostly. They're as different as chalk and cheese. I've seen all his letters. I still see them – and five times he's described his "secret valley".'

'Described it clearly?'

'Not what you'd call precisely. But he's mentioned a few landmarks – and we do know what basic area he fancied.'

'You been back there?'

Dawson looked almost ashamed. 'I can't help it. Sort of an obsession. I've been near a dozen times.'

'And?'

'And the last time, only last week it was, I reckon I found his secret valley, his valley of secrets . . . I was just walking, no method in it. But suddenly I *knew*. It was quiet, and sinister – and I understand Bunscombe's mind as well as anyone can. And I *knew*.'

Dawson stared unseeingly at his empty glass. Barlow had it filled, then asked quietly, 'Shared this knowledge with anybody else?'

'No. Only you.'

'When you going to take another look up there?'

'I will one day.'

'How about tomorrow?'

Jim Dawson gave him a rueful grin. 'Not so fast, Charlie. It was a good few years ago, remember? It's not even in my area anymore.'

'Never mind that. Tomorrow.'

'I can't swing that, Charlie.'

'I can.'

Dawson's hand which had been reaching for the drink paused in mid-air. He looked hard at Barlow. Barlow looked back.

'By tomorrow?'

Barlow nodded. 'I'm having dinner with the Chief tonight.'

He got to his feet and looked at his watch. 'We'd better make it early tomorrow. We don't want any stray hikers poking their noses in. We'll leave at five. Then we'll be up there by the time it's light. Can you get the dogs laid on?'

'Yes.'

Jim Dawson looked a trifle shaken.

'Right. If I'm going to have a five o'clock start and dinner tonight I'm going to get some sleep now.'

'You are sure you can swing it?'

The query was slightly apologetic. But it was still a query.

'Don't worry about that, Jim. You fix the dogs. I'll fix the Chief Constable ... Hang on a minute ...' Barlow stepped back to the table. 'I almost forgot my bowler.'

The track petered out at the foot of a hill and Dawson stopped

the car. 'Uphill all the way now,' he said. 'Hope you're in training.'

Behind, the dog van stopped too. The Sergeant moved to open the rear doors and out came a huge, restless Alsatian followed fast by the sheepdog. They shook gratefully and seemed all set to play. 'Heel,' called the Sergeant and another policeman almost simultaneously, and the dogs fell in obediently.

'PC Swallow, sir,' said the Sergeant. 'And this is Rex.'

'Looks a real dog, that one,' said Dawson.

'At this job they're about equal, sir,' said Swallow. 'And Meg works better with me.'

'She does too,' said the Sergeant without enthusiasm. 'But Rex is a real police dog. Can handle himself chasing villains, and he can sniff out pot too.'

'Very talented,' said Barlow. 'So long as he knows what we want him to sniff out today.'

They stood for a moment looking across the moorland – empty and uninviting in the pale morning light. There was the faint whistle of a curlew sounding far too musical, and then a sheep answered hoarse and miserable and more in keeping with the place. Barlow shivered slightly.

As if in answer, Jim Dawson began to walk. It was soft and springy under foot – peat bog which gave at every step, making the calf muscles ache. Yet although the ground was soft, the surface was covered with stiff earth or wiry tussocks of grass sprinkled with clumps of twisted heather that whipped at their legs. It was a place that didn't welcome intruders and made everyone who walked through it feel like one. The wind was cold.

After two miles Barlow was tired. The dogs loped steadily ahead of them, Meg casting out now and again in a sheepdog's circle, never moving in a completely straight line, always herd-

c

ing invisible sheep. Dawson marched on ahead like a man with an appointment to keep. The dog-handlers were silent, made uneasy by the company they were keeping and the job they were here to do.

Eventually, just as Barlow's pride was losing the battle with his legs, Dawson stopped a few yards ahead and looked down. Barlow drew alongside him. 'This is it.' It was not a valley in the sense any lowland dweller would use the word. Valleys have woods and meadows and a stream running through. They even sometimes have buttercups. This had silence and no stream. It was a long groove in the moorland with a scattering of boulders and at the bottom a huddle of dwarf trees which even in the shelter were bent double by the wind. It made Barlow think of ancient Druids and rites and – he pushed the thought away.

Dawson said nothing. He merely turned to the dog-handlers and nodded. They snapped their fingers and the dogs came to heel. The handlers bent and whispered. It was the same command that Barlow had heard in the field by the training centre, but this time he was near enough to hear the words. There were just two, often repeated: 'Find bod . . . find bod.'

Steadily men and dogs began to move down into the valley. Barlow and Dawson stood still and watched. Suddenly there was a harsh cry. Barlow felt Jim Dawson stiffen alongside him as the grouse jumped out of the heather below them. Rex halted for a moment, then put his nose back to the ground and went steadily on. Meg continued her sweeping circles. Twenty minutes went by and the dogs were still tracking up and down the shallow sides, around boulders and through the trees. Rex was still in sight but Meg was half hidden by the trees before she vanished behind them. Barlow was watching a small brown bird sitting on a rock. It flicked its tail at Barlow in a flirtatious way and then flew across to perch on a low grassy mound.

Barlow was just wondering whether or not it was a skylark when he saw the dog-handler starting to run.

The four of them stood together in silence, staring down into the shallow grave the sheepdog had half uncovered. She and the Alsatian seemed ready again to play. It was Jim Dawson who broke the silence: 'And who the hell is that?'

The body lay on its back with the arms folded neatly across its chest. There was a gun-shot wound in the side of the head. It was the body of a fully-grown man and it had not been in the ground very long.

'Nobody known to you?'

'No sir.' Barlow was not surprised at Dawson's suddenly disciplined response: this was a 'mysterious death' and not in his own territory. He was assuming that Barlow would take charge.

'Right. We'll leave you in charge of the body, Swallow.'

'Yes sir. Can I have the dog too? She might sniff something else out.'

'You can have her for company. But I won't have you straying from here. Now then. Single file please and along this route.'

Barlow headed back the way they had come. 'Got enough of a look for the first message?'

'Just about, sir,' said Dawson.

'No doubt it's outside the county?'

'No doubt, sir,' said the Sergeant. 'A good ten miles outside. I'll get the precise map reference when we reach the van.'

They plodded on, the Alsatian the only one of them enjoying it. Barlow flopped into Dawson's car. 'Let's get drafting.'

In two minutes they had the message complete and Dawson sent out his call-sign, 'Headquarters Eight'. The response was immediate, and Dawson went on: 'I've a message for our

Number 4 District and for Yorkshire HQ. It reads: "At 18.10 hours today, while watching a police-dog exercise on Lowgill Moors Map Ref 74D Det Chief Supt Barlow of the Home Office Research Services Branch and Det Chief Supt Dawson of the Lancashire Constabulary found the clothed body of a man, partly buried in a shallow grave. The man appears to be middle age, slight in build, dark hair. Fuller details will be telephoned to Det Chief Supt Harry Martin at Yorkshire Force HQ. Your best way of reaching the scene by a motor vehicle is travelling along the B6480 from Settle, taking the first farm track on the left after the Dog Inn. I will arrange for a dog-van driver to be at that entrance to escort you to the scene, which is about 1¾ miles from the main road." '

They heard the message repeated, then Dawson swung the car round to head for the nearest telephone. 'Will you tell Harry Martin, sir? I'd like you to.'

Barlow grinned. 'I'll do you a favour any time, Jim.'

Within a few hours the 'secret valley' was full of men. Barlow stood on the crest, watching the murder machine rolling into action. The grave was surrounded by screens. There were two tents within a hundred yards of it. A mobile police station dominated the head of the valley, its telescopic radio aerial trembling slightly in the wind. Barlow saw the mobile canteen lurch along the track and thought of the hot soup that would be ladled out within minutes. But his mind was racing: somewhere, he knew, he had seen the face that had stared up at them from the ground. He didn't know the man. He had never met him. But he knew the face.

Then he remembered. A year ago, when he had become involved in the attempt to hijack nuclear waste, he had been desperately looking for information. A colleague in the Yard had shown him a file of men who dealt in whispers from the underworld. Not regular police informers known only to the

officer who handled them, but men who had information to sell to the highest bidder – a newspaper, the police or another criminal. He was sure that this man's face had been in that file.

Quickly he walked down the hill to tell Dawson and his opposite number Harry Martin. It was Dawson who asked the obvious question.

'What is a bloke who operated in the Smoke doing dead and buried up here?'

His opposite number was more practical.

'We'll send CRO at the Yard his fingerprints. Let's make sure it's him.'

Barlow reached out a hand.

'Don't send them. Give them to me. I'll take them.'

Martin hesitated slightly.

'I'm going to have my Chief agree to let Jim Dawson head this enquiry, Mr Barlow. As far as I'm concerned, he's in charge.'

'And glad to use you as a messenger.' Jim looked at Barlow with just a faint suspicion of a grin on his face. 'One thing, sir . . . don't get hit on the head this time.'

Barlow was icy. 'Let neither of you risk getting kicked in the teeth for not clearing this one up fast.'

It took only a few minutes for Criminal Records to confirm Barlow's suspicions. The inspector on duty pushed a card across towards him.

'That's him alright. Anthony Turner, aged forty-two. Three convictions: petty larceny, living on immoral earnings, money with menaces. Nasty bit of work. I'll telex the good news to the North.'

Barlow asked, 'Who knew him best?'

'Doubt if anybody'd claim credit for that, but it was Brooks

who pulled him in last time. Brooks is a DI at West End Central.'

Barlow eventually found him in 'The Green Lion' on the corner of Greek Street. It was a pub packed to the doors in daytime with the normal Soho assortment of film editors in long hair and tight jeans, advertising men in severe suits and dashing shirts, designed to prove they were both reliable and with-it, and a sprinkling of the area's entertainment industry both male and female. As Barlow pushed the door open he was almost flattened by a burly stripper clutching her vanity case in one hand and a beef sandwich in the other, moving at speed to the next stop on her circuit.

Detective Inspector Brooks proved easy to recognise, largely from the way in which three other men at the bar were trying to pretend that his being there didn't bother them. When Barlow joined him, their apprehension changed to near panic and they drank up and left.

'What's the matter with those three?' asked Barlow after he had introduced himself and bought them both a drink.

'They did the jewellers in Bruton Street. What can I do for you?'

Barlow told him. The Inspector drank steadily from his pint before answering.

'So Tony Turner's dead is he? Well, well ... No tears for Tony. A pair of big ears and a slimy tongue. That was Tony.'

'Did you use him?'

The Inspector looked offended: 'Me? No, not Tony. One or two at the station might have had him on their string. But he wasn't on mine. I like my information straight and simple. Nothing was very simple with Tony and it was never straight.'

'Did he make money?'

'He made a bundle from time to time. There are a couple of crime reporters ... freelances. They used him. "Secrets of the

Soho jungle" – that sort of thing. What the girls were paying and who the landlords were. Good crusading stuff with sex all over it. But he shouldn't be dead.'

Barlow lifted a hand towards the barman. The Inspector waited until their order was front of them.

'Cheers. No. Tony shouldn't be dead. A good kicking up a back alley – that's the treatment for Tony . . . particularly around here. They don't go in for shootings around here – the noise is bad for business.'

'Well, somebody shot him and buried him in the middle of nowhere.'

'That's another thing.' The Inspector looked gloomily around the pub. 'I can't see any of this lot doing that. They don't go for wide open spaces one little bit. They get nervous in the middle of Soho Square. Three quarters of them haven't even heard of Yorkshire, never mind finding it.'

'So not this connection?'

'There must be another. Still, that's your problem. I'll ask around for you. Thanks for the drink. Must go.'

The landlord was just calling 'Last orders' and Barlow pointed to their glasses in enquiry.

'No thanks,' said the inspector with a wintry smile. 'Business before pleasure. I've got to go and pick those three up for the jeweller's job. They'll be next door still. That's the thing about my lot here. Creatures of habit. The one who killed Tony – you won't find him here. Mind you, God knows where you will find him. Still – good luck.'

He nodded and was gone. Barlow stared gloomily after him. His headache had come back.

It was two days later that his phone rang and the gloomy voice of Inspector Brooks floated through the mouthpiece.

'It's about Tony. Just before he disappeared he was talking

to a chap called O'Reilly. He's one of those freelance crime reporters I was talking about. You'll find him in that pub in Fetter Lane – the newish one. He's there every evening until about half past seven.'

Barlow put the phone down with a word of thanks and looked at his watch. There was no point in going home. He would occupy the time with a couple of phone calls to see what information he could glean about Mr O'Reilly. He also phoned Jim Dawson, who was very glum: no one had seen Tony Turner alive in the area; no one had seen a strange car; no one had seen a strange anything. Turner, it seemed, had vanished from his haunts in Soho and been magically transported to turn up dead in a hole on the Yorkshire moors. He had been there it seemed just over three weeks. Since no bullet had been found it was assumed he had been shot elsewhere.

Putting his coat on, Barlow headed for the door. In the taxi to Fetter Lane he ran through again what he had learned about O'Reilly. He was, it appeared, a specialist: hard-bitten, tough, totally unscrupulous in pursuit of what he called 'a story' but which was largely information that could be sold to one or other of the popular Sundays or to a Continental magazine.

Barlow's informant had been unenthusiastic about the whole breed: 'They're vampires and ghouls most of them and they really would sell their grandmothers. There's one man who makes £7,000 a year doing nothing but inventing stories about the royal family and then selling them to *France Dimanche* and rags like that. He never goes anywhere but he knows what they want, so he just sits at home and makes it up. ... O'Reilly doesn't do that. He specialises in crime and the underworld. He comes from the Old Kent Road area and he was at school with the Krays, so he's half in that world anyway. He's very careful not to print anything that would get him into trouble and the boys use him sometimes to get an

enemy nailed. He's good though. Don't make any mistake about that. If he gets onto a story he'll go after it and nothing will stop him getting it. He's the one who nearly got sent down – he and a photographer – for breaking and entering. There was a photograph of a murdered woman in her flat. They knew it was there and one of the Sundays was offering good money for one, so they just broke in and got it.'

Barlow had never had any great love for the press in general and crime reporters in particular. He was looking forward to meeting Mr O'Reilly – who was *not* in the pub in Fetter Lane, and seemingly nowhere else either. Laboriously Barlow traced his office number.

The 'office' admitted to being that of a news agency but its staff were not helpful. When informed by Barlow's secretary that 'the Home Office' would like to speak to Mr O'Reilly, they said he was not available. Mr O'Reilly used the office only very occasionally. Equally, a home number produced a wife whose knowledge of her husband's movements was so vague as to imply either total indifference or total obedience to standing instructions.

After two days of leaving messages Barlow tacked the problem less officially. He had it whispered that Detective Chief Superintendent Barlow would like to buy Mr O'Reilly a drink and discuss a matter of mutual profit.

Within two hours his phone rang.

'Mr Barlow? This is Geoff O'Reilly. You've been trying to find me.'

The voice was flat and totally lacking in emphasis. Barlow fixed a time and a place – at eight that evening in a pub in Cable Street that he had never patronised. He had heard of it, though: it had once been the hang out of some of the more violent associates of the Krays.

Barlow half-wondered why O'Reilly regarded it as a suitable

place to meet – unless he was often seen talking to senior policemen there. Barlow made a note to pass the information on. There was an Assistant Commissioner who would be interested.

He arrived early but spent a pleasant ten minutes gazing at the vast bar. There had been only seven customers when he began his private game of trying to estimate the length of time spent in prison by each. This involved staring throughtfully at them in turn. As a result, three drank up and left. Barlow had just decided on an approximate figure of five years when a voice spoke in his ear:

'You're Barlow. I'm drinking Scotch. What about you?'

Barlow pushed his glass towards the barman, then turned to look at the man who had joined him. O'Reilly's appearance was as undramatic as his voice. Sandy hair neither particularly long nor short, rather colourless, pale-blue eyes, a round face with a slightly snub nose, stockily built without being noticeably broad-shouldered. The impression he gave was of a man trying hard to give as little impression as possible. His raincoat, even, was a perfect compromise between brand-new and shabby. Barlow realised that it would be quite easy to forget that O'Reilly was there – which no doubt O'Reilly found useful.

He nodded to the remaining customers, then taking both drinks moved away to a corner table. Barlow followed.

'You come here often?'

O'Reilly nodded.

'You know the area well then?'

He got another nod in exchange. It was like trying to open a sardine tin with a matchstick.

'Are you from around here?'

'Yes.'

'I thought journalists were supposed to be a talkative lot.'

'Not my sort of journalist.'

'And what sort of journalist is that?'

'You already know. Otherwise you wouldn't want to talk to me.'

O'Reilly picked up his drink, took a sip and sat quietly examining the table in front of him. Barlow allowed the silence to continue. Finally, O'Reilly looked up: 'What can I do for you, Chief Superintendent?'

Barlow glanced over his shoulder. 'I gather you deal in information – information that comes from, shall we say, somewhat unorthodox sources. You don't ask questions and you pay well.'

He waited. O'Reilly took another sip of his drink. Barlow went on: 'I think you might be able to help me. So I asked you to come and have a drink. That's all.'

Barlow got up, went to the bar and came back with two more drinks. O'Reilly nodded an acknowledgement.

'I might be able to help. It depends.'

'Depends on what?'

'What it is . . . And how much you want?'

Barlow fingered his jaw and stared reflectively into the pale-blue eyes that looked back at him.

'How about a list of all the Yard officers who are the subject of confidential investigation at the moment?'

O'Reilly's eyes narrowed as he put his glass down, but his face stayed carefully expressionless. He thought for a moment. 'A thousand.'

'You're in a position to offer that? You wouldn't have to clear it with anyone?'

There was a shake of the head.

'Well,' Barlow rubbed his hands cheerfully together, 'If I ever want to sell that list, I'll make a point of giving you first refusal. In the meantime how about coming down to the station with me?'

'What for?'

'I could charge you with attempting to bribe a police officer.'

If he had been hoping for a dramatic effect he was disappointed. All he got was another shake of the head.

'No?'

O'Reilly sipped his drink again. 'You wouldn't do that.'

'Wouldn't I?'

Barlow had stopped smiling now.

'No evidence.'

'I might not care about that.'

This time O'Reilly didn't shake his head. He just shrugged his shoulders. Barlow leant across and took O'Reilly's elbow in a firm grip. The journalist looked down at the hand that was holding him but made no move to remove it.

'Everything all right, Geoff?'

The threat was unsubtle but unmistakeable. Barlow looked up. One of the men from the bar had come over and was standing beside the table. The question had been addressed to O'Reilly but the man was looking at Barlow. Barlow looked back. Then he spoke softly.

'The National Westminster job in Baker Street.'

The man blinked rapidly and went back to the bar. Barlow turned to O'Reilly. This time O'Reilly did make a move. He took Barlow's hand off his arm. Barlow let him do it.

'Listen, Chief Superintendent, you may think you're a cat. But I'm no mouse. And I've had that trick tried on me before.'

'I thought you might have. I wasn't all that bothered either way.'

O'Reilly got to his feet. 'I'm glad about that. I've also got work to do.'

'Sit down.'

The tone of voice was affable enough. O'Reilly stared hard at Barlow's face. Then he sat down.

'Alright. But make it quick.'

'I want some information.'

'I don't give information.'

Barlow ignored the comment. Instead he reached into his pocket and drew out a photograph. It had been taken while the man was still in the grave.

'I want some information about him.'

'He's dead.'

Barlow felt his temper slipping. He controlled it with an effort. 'You said you had work to do?'

O'Reilly nodded.

'Well, I'm afraid it will have to wait.'

'Why should it?'

'Because you're going North. By train. And it may be too late to start tonight. That means we shan't get together until tomorrow afternoon. It may then be a little while before they get around to questioning you up there. And it may take more than a day. What's today? ... Monday ... You'll be back by Friday.'

'Why?'

Barlow nodded at the photograph. 'You were seen talking to him. For all I know you were the last person to see him alive.' Barlow leant confidentially across the table. 'I think you may have killed him.'

'Are you charging me?'

'No. I'm just sharing my thoughts with you. And it isn't my case. But I feel it is your duty as a citizen to go up there and tell them all you know.'

O'Reilly leant back in his chair, regarding Barlow thoughtfully ... 'Helping the police with their inquiries.'

That's right.'

'And if I don't ... No,' O'Reilly swallowed his drink and

stood up. 'Scrub that. I've got no choice.' He stood looking down at Barlow . . . 'You coming?'

'Where?'

'You tell me. North you said. Leeds or Manchester?'

They left the pub with no word of farewell although Barlow could almost hear an intense silent humming behind. He was, for once in his life, at a loss. His bluff had been called. The implication was that O'Reilly did, in fact, know a great deal about the murder. Barlow was fairly sure that he didn't. But, in that case, why was he prepared to endure the inconvenience and boredom of a long journey and an interrogation which would be a total waste of his time. Unless . . . Barlow stopped on the pavement as a thought struck him – unless O'Reilly had his own reasons for wanting to be kept out of circulation – and safe? He examined the thought for a moment and then rejected it. O'Reilly, he decided, was just being bloody-minded. Very well! He would have to be even more so. The only problem was, he couldn't think how.

O'Reilly had been walking a few yards ahead of him. Now he stopped beside a dark-grey Jaguar.

'A villain's car,' thought Barlow to himself in his bad temper. O'Reilly was reaching into his pocket.

'If you don't mind,' and there was no irony in his voice, 'We'll take this wherever you want to go. I don't fancy leaving it here for four days.'

Barlow nodded and crossed to the passenger side. He stood and waited while O'Reilly found his keys. He fumbled for a second with the door and then got in. Suddenly Barlow felt better.

His voice was as flat as his companion's had been : 'We'll go to the Yard. I expect you know the way.'

O'Reilly glanced up and down the road, swung the car round in a U-turn and headed towards central London. They

had been driving for five minutes and were heading along a fairly empty stretch of road when Barlow reached across and swung the wheel over to the left. Instinctively O'Reilly braked and swung it back

There was a squeal of tyres. Barlow braced himself in his seat. And the car slid gently and inexorably across the road until a front wheel mounted the pavement and, with a loud noise of metal and glass, a front light and wing crumpled against a concrete lamp-post.

'What the. . . ?'

O'Reilly's calm had totally vanished. But Barlow cut in on him, his voice with a new edge to it.

'Right. No more games. You've had an accident. You've been drinking. You're over the limit. And that means a year off the road. Very awkward for a man in your job. We sit here until a patrol car comes past. And they make you blow in the bag. Or you tell me what I want to know. Think about it. You've got ten seconds.'

O'Reilly did not look at Barlow. He leant both hands on the wheel and stared ahead for slightly longer than the allotted time limit. Then he sat back in his seat.

'Alright . . .' His voice, too, had changed. The flat tone had gone. Instead it was rough with anger . . . 'Tony Turner came looking for me. I knew him. I knew what he did. He had a photograph. And he said there was a story that went with it. A big story. He wanted five hundred for it. I offered him fifty. And I sent him away to think it over. He was small time. I didn't think he'd come across anything big. I arranged to meet him two days later. He never turned up. That's all I know.'

'Dates?'

'It was three, no, four weeks ago.' He dug out a diary. 'I saw him on 12 March.'

Barlow almost purred, 'He was found on 5 April. Patho-

logist thinks he'd been buried about three weeks. Say on about 14, 15 March.'

'I never saw him again.'

'He didn't give you any clue what kind of a story it was?'

'No.'

'But he left the picture?'

'One print – or part of one print.'

'I'll have it.'

O'Reilly leant across and unlocked the glove compartment. He took out an envelope and handed it to Barlow without a word. Barlow took it and inspected it in the light from the street lamp which seemed unaffected by the collision.

'And this is all? Nothing else?'

'That's all. He wouldn't say anything else until he saw money.'

Barlow looked at the picture again and turned back to O'Reilly. 'Alright.'

O'Reilly pushed the compartment shut with a vicious snap. 'And now, Chief Superintendent ... get out of my car. And out of my way. And don't ever lean on me again.'

Barlow reached for the door handle. 'You've been very co-operative. So I'll lean back a bit. You have twenty-four hours to go, I'd advise with your solicitor, to any police station to make a formal statement recounting what you've told me. Make sure you do that. And you're at liberty to say that you handed the photograph to Mr Barlow of the Home Office.' He scribbled busily. 'This is my receipt.'

On the pavement he bent down again until he could see O'Reilly's face. 'One piece of advice. Don't try and drive this car with only one headlight. It's against the law and a police-man might stop you.'

Anthony Gordon Fenton, Assistant Secretary at the Home

Office, was intrigued – and admitted as much. He gazed at the photograph Barlow laid on his desk. 'Dear me, Charles, you have been busy. First a body, and now this . . . It is an unusual photograph.'

'Agreed. It's not the kind of happy snap we usually come across in this kind of game. Just two men sitting at a table having a drink together – and both of them with their clothes on.'

Fenton believed in dotting the i's and crossing the t's as he went along. 'Would you care to be more precise about the particular "kind of game" you are referring to?'

'Tony Turner dealt in information. He thought that picture was worth money. He tried to sell it to O'Reilly. O'Reilly wanted more information about the men in the picture and wasn't prepared to fork out until he got it. Turner was coming back to see him again. He never turned up. I think Turner also approached somebody more directly involved. Either one of those two men or someone connected with them.'

Fenton got up and moved towards the cupboard where he kept his sherry. Barlow suppressed a groan. He hated sherry. Perhaps one day, when he knew Fenton a little better, he would suggest an investment in a bottle of Scotch. Fenton turned around with two glasses in his hand: 'And one of those two men or, as you say, someone connected with them did not appreciate Turner's interest in the matter. It is a possible hypothesis.'

'It's what happened. It has to be. That photograph, for some reason, is dynamite. The only trouble is – we don't know why. Because someone, presumably Turner, has very carefully cut both heads out of the picture.'

'Both heads,' said Fenton thoughtfully sipping sherry. He looked across at Barlow and leant forward suddenly.

'Charles, may I ask you a question?'

D

Startled, Barlow nodded.

'Do you really like sherry?'

'No.'

The answer was out before Barlow could collect himself. Fenton got up without a word, took the glass from Barlow's hand and moved to the cupboard. He reached up, removed a copy of *Who's Who* and extracted a bottle of malt whisky from behind it. He poured Barlow a glass and handed it to him.

'That may be more to your taste.'

Barlow accepted the glass and the implied compliment equally gratefully. Fenton sat down and prodded the photograph with a finger.

'Both heads,' he repeated. 'In other words what matters is not just the identity of the two men but the fact that they have been seen together on terms of some intimacy. And one of them is holding a *Times*. You can read the headline. The photographer seems to have taken care to show that. It gives a date.'

Barlow nodded his agreement. It was very good whisky.

'Right,' said Fenton briskly. 'Now, my dear Charles, indulge me. Let me see what a good detective can deduce from that photograph.'

Barlow pulled it towards him. He was silent for a minute and then he started talking slowly, half to himself, half to Fenton: 'Abroad ... Mediterranean somewhere – at least judging by the quality of the light. They aren't in holiday clothes but those are light-weight suits ... There's a lot of ice in those drinks too ... that's a wine bottle between them there ... not Chianti though – slim-necked ... They're drinking on a terrace somewhere ... There's a foot in the picture from another table ... wearing one of those rope-soled things ...'

'That narrows it down a great deal.'

Barlow ignored the sarcasm. 'Wait a minute. You can't see

any label on their bottle, it's turned away. But there's a bottle on the corner of the table behind them. You haven't got a magnifying glass, have you?'

Fenton pulled open a drawer. 'Oddly enough I have. One of my former masters used to write minutes in the most disgusting miniscule handwriting imaginable and a magnifying glass became indispensable.'

Barlow took the glass and peered at the photograph. He bent over until his forehead was almost touching the desk and then straightened, blinking hard. 'I can just about make out the last letters of the word in the middle of the label . . . I-T-E.'

'That should be fairly straightforward. We need to find a wine which is called "Something-ite".'

Fenton reached for a phone. 'Why don't we ring my wine merchant and ask him? On second thoughts . . .'

He replaced the receiver thoughtfully . . . 'He's knowledgeable about port but not particularly well up on plonk. And I have a feeling that what we are in search of is plonk.' He looked at his watch. 'It's ten to six. Have you any engagements within the next hour or so?'

Barlow shook his head.

'Then why don't we go to a rather pleasant wine bar I know – just off Shepherds Market. They should be able to help us and we could have a drink while they did so?'

He caught the slight flicker of surprise on Barlow's face. Fenton worked hard *in* the office but he usually left it fairly promptly, and drinking with the help was not something he normally indulged in. Fenton gave him what in any lesser civil servant would have been described as a grin.

'My wife is away. She has gone to visit her mother.'

Barlow kept his face carefully expressionless. He had never thought of Fenton as having a mother-in-law. Come to that, it

was not until recently that he had even thought of Fenton as having a mother. Nevertheless, he found himself wondering just what was going on as he followed Fenton out of the Home Office and into a taxi. First the whisky and now this. He had a feeling that Fenton had spotted something in that photograph that he himself had missed. He spent the journey wondering just what it could have been.

The wine bar was small and dark with high-backed oak settles and hard benches. It was empty except for an elderly barman with a wrinkled leathery face. He greeted them amiably and Fenton ordered a bottle of Beaune. When it was brought to their corner, Fenton pressed a pound note into the Barman's hand and explained their problem.

'Ending in I-T-E you say, sir?'

'That's right,' said Barlow. 'Mediterranean probably. The kind of drink you'd have a bottle of before lunch and shovel ice into.'

The man looked rather pained. 'I see, sir.'

'We aren't suggesting you stock it,' added Fenton with a smile. 'We just want to know what it might be and where it would come from.'

'I should be able to help you. I'll just go and consult the lists.'

He reappeared almost immediately, triumphantly clutching a catalogue. 'Here we are sir. It didn't sound familiar, not "ite" as in "mite". But a traveller called in some weeks ago. He mentioned a white wine. Here we are. Aphrodite. Rhymes with mighty. 95p a bottle.'

'Never heard of it,' said Barlow. 'Where's it come from?'

'Cyprus, sir. He claimed it was quite pleasant. But I didn't order any.'

He left them alone, staring at each other.

'Cyprus,' said Fenton reflectively. 'You've been there,

Charles? That business of the forged printing plates.'

Barlow nodded.

'Do you fancy going again?'

'It isn't my case,' said Barlow bluntly.

'It is now, my dear Charles.' Fenton leant over and filled Barlow's glass. His voice had grown slightly silky which was always a bad sign. Barlow braced himself.

'It's true the body was found in the North but I think we can assume that the choice of location was fairly arbitrary. The picture holds the key. One of these men is important, probably very important.'

'How can you tell?'

'He was wearing something.'

'They were both dressed. Well dressed, I'd say. Light-weight suits, conservatively cut.' Barlow paused. 'Did I miss one of the ties or something?'

Fenton was indulging but not enjoying his triumph. 'You did miss something. The ties had no message for me but one man's cuff-links did. I spotted, with the aid of the glass, the unmistakeable Y.'

'Why?'

'Because he must be a member. Oh I see. I mean the capital letter Y.'

'Does he belong to the YMCA or what?'

'He belongs, Charles, to the WHY club, spelt W-H-Y. The single capital letter Y is a mild joke.'

'Then why aren't you laughing fit to bust?'

'Because I am concerned, even alarmed. I know very little of the WHY Club except that it meets four or five times a year and that I could barely aspire to membership.'

'Is it that crooked?'

'No Charles. It is that exclusive.'

'Socially? Intellectually? Or is it a millionaires' club?'

'I would have said power rather than wealth was the criterion. There is a sprinkling of dukes, I believe. There may be a millionaire or two.'

Barlow beamed. 'For once you're vague.'

'Inevitably so. There is nothing sinisterly secret about the WHY Club but it is overwhelmingly discreet. One has to be invited to join, of course, then one is vetted very thoroughly, if informally.' Fenton coughed slightly. 'I was given to understand that I should have to rise two whole grades before I could be even considered.'

'That's powerful stuff alright.'

Fenton had recovered. 'So powerful that any possible connection with crime must be traced ... You have a date from *The Times* in the photograph. It is, I believe, essential that you discover, and discover soon, which personage was drinking Aphrodite on a terrace somewhere in Cyprus with an unknown man whom he had no business to be seen with. And that's it.'

He leant elegantly back in his seat, looking pleased with his concise summary. Barlow stared stolidly back.

'Is your wife staying at her mother's?'

Fenton looked slightly startled. 'Yes, as a matter of fact she is.'

'Right.' Barlow waved an arm at the waiter. If he couldn't get even with Fenton, at least he would leave him with a headache.

It was hot at Nicosia airport and customs asked no more than 'No seeds, fresh fruit or vegetables?' But the man at passport control looked hard at Barlow's passport, asked him politely to wait and went away. Barlow sat without anxiety. He had expected the check. Too many of his colleagues had been on Special Branch duties during the EOKA troubles for British

policemen to be totally welcome in Cyprus. There was a black-list, but his name was not on it. His only visit to the island had been four years ago, and then he had cleared up a case of forgery which could have ruined the island. He had been given a ceremonial farewell.

A few minutes later the official came back and returned his passport. He gave Barlow a nod of respect as well as acknowledgement, Barlow gave him a nod in return. He collected the hired car that had been arranged for him. It bore the wide black-and-white band around the side that all tourist cars carried. Travelling by road was even then difficult in Cyprus with the island parcelled up between the Greeks and Turks. Turks manning their road blocks did not allow Greeks through; the Greeks reciprocated. There was only sporadic violence – the two communities merely made life difficult for each other. The island needed tourists – and was careful not to involve them in what was strictly a two-family quarrel. Some of the violence was avowedly token: the United Nations forces provided a lot of money too.

On the road to Kyrenia Barlow saw ahead the long line of cars escorted by two pale-blue jeeps with headlights blazing. This was the daily procession of Greek cars being escorted through the Turkish strip that separated them from the town. The other way round was lengthy, so each day the United Nations peace-keeping force ran this official gauntlet. Barlow slowed down and tagged on behind. In Kyrenia itself he turned off and headed along the coast road for a mile until he found the sign he was looking for: the Palm Court Hotel. Within five minutes he was comfortably settled behind the bar exchanging gossip and whisky sours with the owner.

Bill Humphreys was a former army officer. He was also the son of a landed Ulster family who happened to be Catholic, which perhaps gave him some insight into the feuds of the

island he had made his home. Barlow had met him on his previous visit. Humphreys had been in the army during 'the Troubles', serving as an intelligence officer. He had then been seconded to the United Nations and eventually decided to stay on as a hotel-keeper. His past involvement had never been held against him by the locals, probably because Bill made it quite clear that he preferred their company to that of the colony of expatriate British in the town. He also resolutely refused to take sides. His hotel was in Greek territory but three miles up the hill was Turkish. Bill talked to both and both were welcome in the bar – provided they left their differences outside. They always did.

The hotel was small and comfortable. Barlow had chosen it because he liked it and he liked Bill. He also knew that Bill could be relied upon to provide intelligent help in confidence.

They gossiped for a while and then Bill reached under the bar and took out a slip of paper: 'Message for you. From a bloke called Fenton. He asked me to write it down. Careful fellow.'

'Civil servant,' said Barlow.

'Not a stupid one though, by the sound of him. Here you are – word for word: "Tell Barlow I have studied our man's portrait again and I have an uneasy feeling that he is a master of his subject." Mean something to you?'

Barlow drank the rest of his whisky sour very slowly and then took a careful lick at the sugar around the glass.

'Yes, Bill, I'm afraid it does. Did he say anything else?'

'Not really. We chatted for a bit. He picked my brains about the situation here. He also gathered I knew you fairly well and he gave me another message which he said I didn't have to write down.'

'What was that?'

'It was, "Tell Barlow to stop knocking back whisky sours

and get on with it." That isn't quite how he put it but the meaning was the same.'

Barlow grinned. 'He's just jealous. It's raining in London. One more, plus a slice of your wife's smashing moussaka. Then to work. Tell me where that is.'

He threw the picture across the bar. Bill picked it up and stared at it. Typically, he did not ask any questions. Then he shook his head: 'Could be anywhere . . . except I'd be inclined to guess that it's Kyrenia area or Nicosia rather than down south in Famagusta or Limasol. I don't know why. It's just a feeling.'

Barlow took the picture back. 'Would you do something else for me?'

'Anything.'

'Get me a list of all the bars that serve Aphrodite wine.'

'It will be a long list. It's a popular brand, particularly round here. Otello for red, Aphrodite for white.'

'I have feet.'

'You're going to need them.' Bill peered over the bar. 'And something more comfortable to put them in. Walk around Kyrenia like that and you'll have all the old tabbies from Torquay stopping and asking you the time.'

'I'll go and change.'

Barlow was half way out of the bar when Bill's voice stopped him.

'It's none of my business. But why isn't your other man staying here? Are you pretending you don't know each other?'

'What other man?'

'He rang up this morning . . . asked for you – by name and rank. I said you hadn't arrived yet. He told me he was working with you . . . Isn't he?'

Barlow slowly shook his head. 'Only two people knew I was coming to Cyprus. You – and the bloke called Fenton.'

The two of them stared blankly at each other. It was Bill Humphreys who cracked first.

'So who was it who phoned here?'

'I haven't the faintest idea. I just hope that I get to find out.'

At least it was a nice day for looking for a needle in several haystacks. Barlow sat on the terrace of a cafe which was not the one he was looking for and considered the problem. He had two things to go on: the photograph identified a place; the newspaper in the photograph implied a date. Barlow decided the place would have to come first. If he were faced with an inspection of hotel registers, then he would prefer to have his choice narrowed down to Limasol or Famagusta or Kyrenia first. Nicosia he ruled out. That photograph had been taken near the sea.

On the other hand, of course, there was no reason why his two anonymous subjects should not have been staying in Limasol and driven up to Kyrenia for the day – or *vice versa*. They might even have been visiting Paphos to inspect the birthplace of Venus but staying in the Troodos Mountains ... come to think of it that photograph could well have been taken on the verandah of that restaurant at Paphos which had the live pelican sitting on its steps.

Barlow decided he needed some help. He got up and moved into the back of the cafe in search of a phone. Within a few minutes he was talking to the Greek police headquarters in Nicosia. An hour later he was just finishing the last few drops of his bottle of wine – Otello appropriately enough – when a car halted at the kerb and a slim elegant policeman got out. The last time the two of them had met they had been chasing two forgers through an olive grove. Aristide was a good policeman. He also had the great virtue in Barlow's eyes of appreciat-

ing that Barlow was a better one.

They exchanged some reminiscences and then Barlow produced his photograph and outlined his problem. Aristide took it and began to laugh. Barlow waited patiently until he had finished and then raised an eyebrow at him.

'It is as well you contacted me, Mr Barlow. You could have looked for this particular cafe for a very long time.'

Barlow's eyebrow stayed raised. Aristide leant forward still smiling and pointed across the harbour at another cafe some two hundred yards away.

'That is the place you seek, Mr Barlow.' He raised a hand to still Barlow's protest although Barlow had not in fact made one. 'I know. You are going to say it does not look at all similar. But that photograph was taken some while ago. Recently, very recently, the cafe has had – I believe the phrase is – a face-lift? The paint is still wet in places.'

Barlow beamed broadly on his slim companion. Then he raised a hand to the waiter. 'Bring us another bottle.'

Once the waiter had gone he pulled his chair nearer to the table. 'Right. Now I have a date on which two men were sitting there. For some reason the fact that they were seen sitting together greatly interested a third person who thought that the information was worth money. He appears to have been correct since someone else thought it was worth killing him. If that is the case it is unlikely that those two men had been here often before, or even stayed together very long. It also seems probable that they arrived separately . . . Can you let me have a list of all arrivals in the week before that picture was taken? And I'll need a list of where each claimed to be staying.'

'Certainly.'

Aristide looked at his watch.

'You shall have it by this evening. I will now make a phone

call to that effect. I shall then return and assist you to finish the wine.'

Barlow leant comfortably back in his chair and watched him go. Then he reached for his glass. He spared a brief thought for Fenton sitting at his desk watching the rain fall in Whitehall and then drank – deeply and with great contentment.

Two days later he was sitting in the same cafe ... in a rage. His inquiries had got precisely nowhere. Aristide had produced the lists as requested. The names had all been checked. Two gentlemen who had signed their hotel registers as Smith had been investigated. That morning Barlow had received a telephone call from Fenton: both of the Smiths were really called Smith, so were the two Joneses and the one Brown.

Fenton had not been encouraging. The murder investigation was at a total standstill. O'Reilly had dutifully made his statement at Cannon Row Police Station. It had been forwarded to the North. The rest was a nothing.

The only 'something' Barlow sensed rather than saw: he believed he was being followed, his steps dogged all over the island. He had not spotted anyone, but he was still sure he was being tailed.

A shadow fell across the table. Barlow looked up to see Aristide standing above him, looking suitably sympathetic – which made Barlow feel even angrier. He waved grumpily at a chair, then glared irritably around him. He sensed again that someone was watching him. He shrugged it away and turned to Aristide.

'Nothing?'

'Nothing ... If only you could give us more to go on, my friend.'

'I don't have any more.'

'But these two men ... who would they be? What kind of men?'

'I don't know. Damn it all, if I knew that, I wouldn't have needed help in the first place.'

Barlow flapped a hand in apology at his own irritation. Then a thought struck him: 'Aristide, would any of your people have been checking on me at my hotel?'

'No.'

'You are sure?'

'I am positive, my friend. For some British policemen – yes. Memories are long here, as you well know. But not for you. To quote the words of that gentleman whose wine you are drinking, "You have done the state some service".'

It was an elegant reminder. Barlow beckoned to a waiter and a second glass arrived. As he poured him a drink, Barlow told Aristide about the phone call to the hotel and his strange feeling that someone was keeping an eye on him. They both automatically glanced around the harbour. No one appeared the slightest bit interested in them.

Aristide was looking embarrassed. 'You see, my friend, these men of yours . . .' Barlow knew what was coming. '. . . They could be staying in the hotels. We have checked those. But one or both of them could be staying in a villa. There are thousands of those all over the island. It could be a villa they own or one they have hired. We have checked arrivals on the London flights, but they may not have come from London. They may not even have come by air. There are twenty yachts in this harbour alone. Without more information . . .'

His voice tailed away. Barlow leant forward and filled his glass. 'I know, Aristide. I can't expect you to keep your men on it any longer. I'm grateful for the help you've given me already. Unfortunately, I have no more information.'

'I am glad that you understand. If it were left to me . . .'

His shrug encompassed a whole world of 'superior officers'. Barlow nodded sympathetically and tried to look more cheerful than he felt.

'What will you do?'

'Go back to London. Report that I've found nothing. Put it away in a file marked "Too difficult".'

Barlow was reaching for the bottle of wine when Aristide's hand closed over his.

'You spoke of being followed.'

'Yes?'

Barlow had not moved but suddenly he was totally alert.

'There is a car parked just in front of the castle wall. It has been there some minutes now. From time to time I have seen the sun glinting inside it. I think there is someone using field-glasses and looking this way.'

Barlow pushed his chair back slowly. 'Perhaps we should go and have a word with them. Can they get out the other way?'

'No. Stay where you are.' Aristide stood up. 'I have a better idea. There is no need for us to disturb ourselves. I will go and ask the waiter to bring another bottle.'

In a few minutes he was back.

'I was able to take a closer look. There is one person in the car – and field-glasses. They may just be watching the ships but I do not think so. They are being held very steadily – and they are pointing straight at this table. In a few minutes we shall know.'

The two of them sat in silence, Barlow resisting the temptation to turn around and watch whatever was happening behind him. Then Aristide gave a small grunt of satisfaction. 'Good. They have him.'

A short while later, a police sergeant threaded his way through the tables. He saluted Aristide and handed him a

folded slip of paper. Aristide read it carefully, his face expressionless. Then he looked across at Barlow.

'I think this is something you attend to personally.'

Barlow looked a startled inquiry.

'It is a matter outside my authority . . . well outside.'

As Barlow continued to stare at him in bafflement, Aristide got to his feet, saluted smartly and marched away. The sergeant flicked a salute at Barlow and followed him. Barlow turned slowly and looked behind him. The car was still there. But as far as he could tell there was now nobody in it.

He got to his feet, tucked some money under a saucer on the table, and started to walk towards the car. Carefully he scanned the walls on either side. There was no one in sight. He walked steadily on. The car was local – no black-and-white tourist stripe. It was also empty, unless whoever was inside had slid down out of sight.

Barlow looked towards the end of the castle wall. Whoever had been there could have ducked around the corner. But why should they have bothered? He stood beside the empty car and looked inside. There were a pair of sun glasses on the dashboard and a packet of local cigarettes. He was about to try the door when a voice behind him.

'And just what do you expect to find in there, Detective Chief Superintendent?'

Barlow closed his eyes. He had not heard that voice for three years.

Slowly he turned round and looked at the slim figure standing behind him. She was as beautiful as ever. Black hair drawn back from her face, dark eyes staring at him, a mouth just a little too wide, curved into half a smile. A cotton dress with a wide skirt gave only a hint of the beautiful body beneath it . . . Despina – a ridiculous name, but for a few brief days Barlow

had been more than a little in love with her. He had been
married then. He was a widower now. He had gone away and
never written. That had been understood. He had forgotten
just how lovely she was. He had been staring at her for a very
long time.

The half smile was still there – amused but slightly cool.

'After three days I thought perhaps I would come and find
you.'

'How did you know I was here?'

He had blurted the stupid question out before he could stop
himself. He got the answer he deserved . . . a faintly incredulous lift of the eyebrows.

'You have forgotten a great deal, Mr Barlow.'

He hadn't. At seventeen Despina had seduced a British
sentry from his post: the sentry had been killed; she had been
caught and imprisoned. With the departure of the British, she
had, she claimed, abandoned all interest in politics, but when
Barlow first met her, four years ago, her network of 'friends'
remained the best on the island. It probably still was, so she
would have been told the moment he landed in Cyprus.

'I haven't forgotten what I used to call you.'

'A long time ago.'

'Still we could have a drink together?'

'That would be very nice.'

She had accepted but her voice had been polite, neutral.
She could have been talking to her bank manager. They
walked down towards the cafe in silence. Barlow knew that it
was up to him. He knew, too, that he was going to let the
challenge go by. The defeat of the last two days was lying too
heavily over him.

He raised his glass to her while he searched for something to
say. The words arrived lamely . . . 'I'm glad you found me.'

'It is not difficult to find anyone on this island.'

Barlow grinned wryly: 'That's what you think.'

'Not if you want to find them.'

Barlow didn't reply. He saw little point in sparring. He was too far behind on points. Instead he turned his head and looked out over the harbour.

'You won't find the answer there. He didn't come by sea.'

He swung back to find Despina sitting back in her seat, looking mockingly at him over the top of her glass.

'You know, Charles, you have changed. A few moments ago, looking at you, I would have said that you looked as if you had given up. And that is not how I remember you at all.'

Barlow leaned forward and took her glass from her hand. He filled it to the brim and handed it back to her. Then he filled his own and raised it to her: 'Your very good health. I will not pretend that I came here to see you – or that I have been looking for you. I haven't. I have been looking for a man – two men – and I haven't found them. But I hadn't forgotten you. I could never do that.'

'A most charming and businesslike speech, Detective Chief Superintendent.'

'You wouldn't have believed any other kind.'

'That is true.'

'Now,' Barlow leant forward. 'You knew I was here. Did your friends tell you why I was here?'

'They told me you were trying to find the identity of two men who were here some time ago.'

'Can you help?'

'I might be able to. But, Detective Chief Superintendent . . .' the voice was no longer totally mocking, '. . . why should I?'

Barlow looked down at the table and then up at the girl. The next answer would be very important.

'Because . . . because you and your friends owe Detective

Chief Superintendent Barlow a small debt. I am asking that it be repaid ... And ... and because Charles Barlow needs help.'

There was a silence and Despina laughed. 'But who could resist an appeal like that...? from Charles Barlow, I mean. Very well. There is a man who visits here occasionally. He has a villa in the hills behind Five Mile Beach. I do not know whether he was here at the time you are interested in. But I think he is the kind of man you should be interested in.'

'Why?'

'My friends, as you know, take an interest in people who come here. We like to know, if only so that we can eliminate those who do not directly concern us. We know nothing against this man. But we also could find out very little about him. He calls himself Thompson. He arrives always from Rome. He never mixes with anyone. Occasionally he has guests. They are invariably men and they arrive only for a few days. He never has parties or guests who come just to enjoy themselves, and yet he is obviously rich. We think he is almost certainly either some kind of shady financier or a criminal. And presumably the men you are looking for are criminals?'

'One of them might be.'

Barlow explained quickly. Despina stood up.

'You will need a photograph of this man.'

'Can you get me one?'

'It is possible. I know someone who keeps such things. Usually he discards those that are of no interest. He may not have done so in this case.'

'When can I see it?'

Despina looked down at him for a moment. Then she laughed: 'Dear Detective Chief Superintendent, so single-minded.'

Barlow felt himself going slowly and maddeningly red. He

looked up like an apologetic grizzly bear and saw her looking down at him. For the first time, her smile wasn't mocking. She bent quickly and he felt her lips brush the top of his forehead.

'You can see it this evening—after you have taken me out to dinner. I am a businesswoman, remember? And in business it is always payment in advance.'

Barlow watched her walk towards the harbour – an enjoyable experience which the other men in the cafe were sharing. Then he sat upright. He had better check if any of Despina's friends had been following him. He got up, threw some money on the table and ran after her. She heard his footsteps and stood beside the car waiting for him. Rapidly he asked and got a very cool denial. So he opened the car door: 'Let's find out who it is then . . . Not too fast. And slow down as soon as you can round the corner.'

She did as she was told. Barlow slid out of the car and pressed himself into one of the embrasures in the castle wall. Within less than a minute a tourist car took the corner sharply. Barlow had a glimpse of a fair-haired man in dark glasses before the car disappeared around the back of the castle. Barlow ran after it and Despina pulled out from the castle entrance where she had tucked her car away.

'Not too close.'

As they turned the corner they saw the car just ahead of them. It had slowed down as the driver obviously tried to work out where his quarry had gone. Then, as if he had made his mind up, he drove slowly on into the centre of Kyrenia. Despina followed gently behind. Whoever was ahead of them circled around the town twice and then drove towards the large modern hotel near the harbour. When they passed they saw it in the car park – empty.

'Alright, love, and thank you.'

Barlow got out.

'I'll pick you up this evening,' said Despina. 'Seven o'clock. And you will be available, won't you, Chief Superintendent?'

Barlow grinned at the threatening tone and waved a reassuring hand. He watched the car drive away and turned towards the hotel. Usually before, when he had been followed, he had known who was on his tail and why. This time he had not the faintest idea ... which at least made an interesting change. He began to walk through the lobby in search of the man with fair hair.

He nearly missed him altogether. But just as he was beginning to think his quarry had retreated to a bedroom, he noticed a few tables set in a small paved area off to one side. There, sitting drinking a lager, with his sun-glasses off and reading a copy of the *Daily Mail*, was ... the journalist O'Reilly.

Barlow turned away in search of a phone. Aristide was not in his office but his assistant expressed his eagerness to be of service to Mr Barlow. Mr Barlow had only to state his request. Mr Barlow did so. There was a slightly startled silence at the other end. But it was followed rapidly by a polite recovery ... But certainly. And when would Mr Barlow like this service performed? Within half an hour? It would be done. For how long would the service be required... ? Mr Barlow would inform them subsequently? That was understood.

Barlow put the phone down and strolled back towards the garden. A quarter of an hour later O'Reilly looked up as a shadow fell across his newspaper. His eyes widened slightly but he motioned towards the other chair : 'Be my guest.'

Barlow sat down. He beamed at O'Reilly with expansive goodwill. 'Do you mind if I ask you a question?'

He got no reaction at all. His smile grew even broader. 'How did you know I was in Cyprus?'

O'Reilly looked thoughtful for a moment. 'I don't see why I shouldn't tell you. I reckoned there had to be a bloody good

story in that photograph to drag you into it. You were the only lead I had. So I followed you. In London you and that other bloke went into that wine bar. I waited until you left and went in after you. I didn't even have to ask the old barman. He couldn't wait to tell me about these two strange men who'd walked in and started asking about wines ending in "ite" and Cyprus. So I got on a plane.'

'And waited for me this end . . . Very clever. And the hotel?'

'It was the fourteenth I'd phoned.'

'Well, well.' Barlow was almost purring with appreciation. 'We could have used you in the Force, Mr O'Reilly. I've rarely come across such initiative and ingenuity. And you've been following me around ever since, hoping I would lead you straight to whatever it is you think is here . . . following me very well too. I didn't spot you at once. But what if I told you I was here on holiday – a sudden impulse – and that that gentleman and I were having that conversation just to settle a bet?'

O'Reilly merely looked contemptuous.

'You wouldn't believe me? No, I didn't think you would. Pity about that.'

Barlow heard heavy footsteps behind him. Two grim looking policemen arrived at their table. They ignored Barlow. One of them spoke to O'Reilly.

'You are Mr O'Reilly?'

'Yes.'

There was a mixture of puzzlement and vague alarm on O'Reilly's face.

'The car you are driving is parked in the front of this hotel?'

'Yes.'

'You will come with us please. You are under arrest.'

'I'll be damned if I will.'

O'Reilly began to settle himself more firmly into his chair. Two large gloved hands wrenched him roughly out of it. In his

rage all he could find was the standard objection: 'What's all this about?'

Barlow looked up at him. His face was very stern. 'I'm afraid you have some explaining to do, Mr O'Reilly.'

'Look!' O'Reilly stabbed a finger at Barlow. 'You can't do this. All I've been doing is driving around this island just like any other tourist.

'Oh it isn't that.' Barlow contrived to look hurt and reproachful. 'Surely you don't think I'd have you thrown into jail just for that? No, of course not.' He looked blandly straight into O'Reilly's eyes. 'No. You see ... They've found a gun in your car.'

'But that's ridiculous.'

Barlow got to his feet, looking bored. 'Show him.'

The small procession made its way to the car park. Without a word one of the policemen opened the door of O'Reilly's car and reached a hand into the side pocket. The hand came up with a gun in it. O'Reilly stared blankly, then turned and swore at Barlow, who looked even more bored.

'It may turn out to be an unfortunate misunderstanding. In which case no harm will be done. But you can understand that with all their troubles, they are a bit sensitive about this kind of thing ...'

He gave a friendly nod to the policemen and walked away, looking at his watch. He had time to bath and change before going to meet Despina.

If Detective Chief Superintendent Barlow found it hard to sit through dinner with his curiosity unsatisfied, Charles Barlow did not mind too much. Despina simply insisted on enjoying the meal without 'boring talk about crime'. They were eating *mezes*, the elaborate Greek hors d'oeuvres that continue for as long as the stomach will hold out.

Barlow's had finally begun to protest. He sat nursing a glass of retzina and looking at Despina. It was a pleasant sight but the policeman was beginning to come to the surface. Despina could sense the struggle.

Her eyes were laughing at him now as her hand hovered over the dish of taramasalata in front of her.

'Shall I just have a little more of this, Charles, or do you think we should say that dinner is now over?'

Barlow refused to rise to the fly. 'My dear, dinner will not be over for some time yet. I seem to remember you made a point of never rising from the table until you had eaten at least three very sticky pieces of baclava and then filled up the cracks with turkish delight.'

She laughed and withdrew her hand. Reaching behind her she produced her shoulder bag and took out an envelope.

'You have been very patient, Charles, sitting there like a sheepdog. Here is your reward.'

Barlow looked at the envelope on his plate. For a moment he was tempted to leave it there unopened. A further moment's thought made him realise that it would be a totally pointless gesture which would convince nobody, least of all Despina. He picked it up and extracted the print inside. Despina saw him stiffen, then he took from his pocket the print of the headless men.

Very carefully he compared the two. There was no doubt. Despina's photograph had been taken from a greater distance but it was sharp enough for Barlow to be able to compare the set of shoulders, the identical clothes. One of the two headless ones he knew.

'They are the same?'

'Yes.'

'Do you know him?'

'Oh yes,' said Barlow thoughtfully. 'I know him very well.'

He looked across hesitantly at her. 'Despina . . .'

She picked up her bag and slung it over her shoulder as she got to her feet. 'I know, Detective Chief Superintendent, you want a telephone. I will run you back to your hotel.'

He tried to avoid looking grateful for her understanding. She caught the struggle on his face and her smile was a trifle rueful.

'Do not worry. I understand. Criminals and ladies do not mix well. I learnt that last time.'

'I don't . . .' Barlow started to speak but she held up a hand and stopped him.

'No, dear Charles, don't tell me that you don't deserve me. Otherwise I might believe you.'

She stopped outside the hotel. Barlow sat for a moment alongside her. Then he leant over and kissed the dark hair where it swept back from her forehead. 'Tomorrow evening. Six o'clock?'

She gave him a mock salute. 'Certainly sir.'

'In the cafe by the harbour?'

This time he got a smile. 'Go and make your telephone call. Do you want me to find out anything more about this man?'

Barlow shook his head. 'No. There is enough known about him. In London there is a file six inches thick.'

He was through to Fenton within half an hour. The calm unruffled tones sounded grumpy. This, it emerged, was due to the fact that it had taken two and a half hours to get from Victoria to Esher. It was also raining. Barlow tactfully refrained from describing his own evening.

'I can put a name to one of our heads, sir.'

The grumpiness disappeared. 'Anyone we know, Charles?'

'Yes. Your friend and mine – Mr Meadows.'

There was silence at the other end. Then – very crisply –
'Sure, Charles?'

'Positive, sir.'

'What about the other one?'

'Nothing yet. And no lead either.'

Fenton's voice took on the rather languid tone it always did
when he was about to impart vital information. 'I think you
should try and find one, Charles. It appears from what you say
that one of those heads belongs to the most powerful organiser
of criminals that this country possesses. And you and I know
that Mr Meadows never does anything without a very good
reason. I've no more idea than you who that second man is. I
can only repeat, if he is wearing those cuff-links legitimately
then he is, by definition, among what a recent television
programme referred to as "the highest in the land". He is also,
in theory anyway, above both suspicion and reproach.'

'What about the list of members?'

Fenton gave a very small sigh. 'It isn't that kind of club,
Charles.'

Barlow's fist clenched around the phone. 'Sir, I don't care
what kind of club it is. They can have black masses in St Paul's
for all I'm bothered. I've been tramping this island and so have
a lot of other people and we haven't found anything because
we don't know what we're looking for. We must have a list of
names.'

Fenton seemed unperturbed by the outburst. 'I can only
repeat, Charles, that it isn't that kind of club. They don't have
"lists" as you put it. However, a gentleman who is a member
has promised to compile one for me.'

'Well ring him up and tell him to get on with it.'

'Why don't you ring him, Charles. I'll give you the number.'
There was a few seconds' pause and then Fenton's voice

recited a series of digits. They were vaguely familiar.

'But that's . . .'

'Precisely,' Fenton cut in on him with silky courtesy. 'So do bear with me, Charles . . . And Charles?'

'Yes, sir?'

'Find that name.'

The phone went down with a click, leaving Barlow staring at the wall. The number Fenton had given him had been the Cabinet Office at Number Ten.

'Have you finished . . . ?'

The international operator's voice broke his trance. The moment the line had been cleared he began to dial again. The phone was answered quickly.

'Aristide.'

'Yes, Charles.'

'Whatever you were doing tomorrow, forget it. And the day after.'

'I am at your service, Charles.'

If Aristide objected to such peremptory commands he was careful not to reveal it. 'What do you have in mind?'

'We are going round the hotels.'

'But my dear Charles, we have already . . .'

Barlow cut in ruthlessly. 'We're going round them again. You and me. Every hotel, every agency, every car-hire firm.'

'It has become very important, Charles?'

'Yes, Aristide. It has become very important indeed.'

'Alright, Charles. I will call for you at seven . . . But you have forgotten something?'

Barlow was startled: 'What?'

'Your friend, the journalist?'

'I had forgotten.'

'He began to become tiresome. Such shouting . . .'

'So what did you do?'

'I had no option.'

'What did you do?'

'There is no cause for concern. I had him declared *persona non grata*. He will be on the midnight plane. That is satisfactory?'

'Very. See you at seven.'

Barlow put down the phone and got ready for bed. It looked as if tomorrow was going to be a very long day. For a few seconds he thought of Despina. He would have to remember to phone her and that would undoubtedly be the end of that.

'Schrabin, de Lanvin, Murphy ... Murphy...? No. A New York address ... Heinemann ... possible ... No. Hamburg ... Greek, Greek ... Vincenzi ... Over to the next page.'

For the first time Barlow was grateful for the economic crisis: it was keeping the number of British tourists within reasonable proportions. He closed the register with a snap. Aristide raised an eyebrow: 'Nothing?'

Barlow shook his head. 'Nothing. At least, I don't think so. Three names. I've made a note – and we'll have them checked again. All I know is that this man's important. But important how? He could be the head of Harwell or the deputy chairman of ICI.'

'But you don't think so, Charles?' asked Aristide shrewdly.

Barlow straightened an aching back. 'No, I don't. I think I'll know the name when I see it. I've no idea what Mr Meadows is doing with this gentleman. But I have a feeling that when I come to the right name, then somewhere a bell is going to ring. Come on. Next one.'

They walked outside and Barlow turned to look back the way they had come. They were in Famagusta. There were twelve modern hotels strung along the seafront. They had

covered every one of them. They had been through the books
of five car hire firms and six agencies. They had some thirty
English names. But Barlow was sure his man's was not among
them. It was twelve o'clock. Next stop Nicosia. They travelled
by helicopter ... courtesy of the United Nations.

It was five o'clock that afternoon when they walked into the
car-hire firm. It was a small one with just one man behind the
counter. As usual, Aristide explained. He outlined the period
of time they were interested in and the man produced a
grubby ledger. Without much hope Barlow bent over it.
During the whole month there had been two English names,
both with London addresses: J. Moore and – Barlow paused.

He stared down at the second name: Wilkinson. Christian
name Christopher. A Cyprus address that sounded like an
apartment block, not a hotel. A London address listed too. He
had hired a Fiat for a fortnight. That seemed to imply that he
had arrived on holiday and not merely to keep an appointment
with Mr Meadows. And yet ... something was trying to
struggle to the surface in his memory. He could hear a voice
for some reason. A voice speaking in a measured tone. There
was also a dim recollection of police orders.

He looked up and saw Aristide staring at him: 'You have
something, Charles?'

Suddenly Barlow remembered. He took Aristide by the
arm: 'Get me to your office and to a phone. I want the fastest
connection with London you can manage.'

Within twenty-five minutes he was speaking to Fenton.
'That list you mentioned, sir. Has it reached you yet?'

'I have an incomplete one, Charles I've been promised any
remaining names by tomorrow. Why? Do you have a
candidate?'

'I'm not sure.' Now that he was about to share the thought
with someone else, Barlow felt oddly diffident. He had no basis

for his assumption – only an instinct that he was right. And that could well be purely a reaction to so many wasted days.

'Try me, Charles.'

Fenton sounded unusually sympathetic as if he sensed what was going through Barlow's mind. Barlow took a deep breath.

'Is the name Wilkinson on it ... Sir Christopher Wilkinson?'

There was no reaction from Fenton. 'Hold on a moment. I'll just check.'

Barlow could see the calm figure sitting behind the desk, running a forefinger carefully and meticulously down the page.

'Charles?'

'Yes.'

'The name is there. Address?'

Barlow gave it to him.

'I'll look him up in *Who's Who*.'

There was another, longer, silence . . .

'It's the same one, Charles. But . . . I can't see what possible interest he could be to Mr Meadows. Can you?'

'No,' said Barlow slowly. 'I can't.'

Fenton said nothing – for so long that Barlow was about to ask if he was still there. Then he spoke – briskly and in his normal style.

'Charles, whenever you and I disagree, which we tend to do fairly frequently, you always at some stage in the proceedings remind me that you are a policeman. Alright, Charles – as a policeman – there is only an unthinkable connection. But, do you feel he is our man?'

Barlow took a very deep breath. 'Yes, sir. I do.'

'In that case, when is the next plane out of there?'

Barlow fired the question at Aristide.

'There's one at seven o'clock.'

'Get on it. There'll be a driver this end.'

Barlow hung up slowly. Aristide was already on the other phone asking to be connected with the airport. There was a rapid exchange of Greek and he looked across at Barlow.

'There is a seat available. I will have someone bring your luggage from Kyrenia.' He replaced his receiver and looked at his watch. 'You have plenty of time. Shall we have a small farewell drink?'

Barlow looked at his watch. It was ten to six. He had forgotten to make his phone call. 'Do I have time to get from here to Kyrenia and then to the airport?'

Aristide grinned in sudden comprehension. 'Yes. You will have to be very quick though. I'll get you a driver.'

Two minutes later Barlow was on his way to the harbour. He did not know what Aristide had said to the driver but he drove like a man inspired or under dire threat. At twenty minutes past six the car skidded to a halt alongside the harbour wall. Barlow got out and walked towards the cafe. The sun was half in his eyes but he could not see Despina at any of the tables. He turned and went inside. A waiter approached him: 'May I help you, sir?'

Barlow looked past him. There was no one there. 'No thank you. I was looking for a friend of mine.'

'A lady, sir?'

'Yes,' said Barlow reluctantly. 'A lady.'

'There was a lady here earlier, sir. She arrived just before six and sat at that table out there.' The waiter hesitated for a moment ... 'A very attractive lady, sir ... She waited for about a quarter of an hour. Then she left.'

'Thank you.' Barlow turned and began to walk back towards the car. The waiter ran after him.

'Any message, sir. Perhaps she will come back.'

'No,' said Barlow. 'No message.'

Fenton noticed that the blotting paper on his desk was not quite straight. With an irritable tightening of the lips he pushed it into its proper alignment and waited for his phone to ring. Eventually it did and a voice at the other end told him what he had wanted to know. He made a careful note of the information and then dialled out himself instead of putting the call through the switchboard. It was to the Ministry of Defence. The telephone was answered by a gentleman who held a comparatively high military rank but was invariably addressed as 'Mr'. Fenton apologised politely for bothering him : 'However, I have a task which falls somewhat outside the capabilities of my people here.'

There was a cautious grunt from the other end. Fenton pressed on : 'A gentleman in whom we have a possible interest is attending a formal dinner this evening. I would like him photographed, preferably seated and holding a glass in his hand. There will be press photographers there, but he is not likely to warrant their attention. So could one of your men oblige?'

The voice at the other end said it thought that could be managed : 'We have an arrangement with one of the posh Sundays. Who is your man?'

Fenton told him.

'Dear me,' said the voice. 'Why do you want a picture of him pouring claret into himself? Blackmail against your old age?'

'If you could oblige me I would be very grateful.'

There was a chuckle. 'It shall be done. When do you want them?'

'Tonight. Another reason I'm asking for your assistance. I do need them urgently', said Fenton. 'Here please. My signature as receipt.'

'Before midnight,' said the voice and put the phone down.

Fenton looked at his watch. There was nothing more he could do now except wait for Barlow ... unless ... he smiled to himself. There was no reason why he should not do a little detective work as well.

Half an hour later he walked into the Garrick Club. Unlike a good many clubs, the Garrick assumes and, indeed, expects that its members will talk to each other. Fenton headed towards the bar, where a prominent QC who specialised in major criminal cases was entertaining a circle of fellow members with some of the more remarkable alibis he had been instructed by clients to offer. Fenton chose his moment and neatly eased him away on a wave of laughter. They retired to a corner and Fenton began, very discreetly, to ask questions.

The two photographs lay side by side on the desk. Barlow and Fenton stared at them in silence. Barlow had arrived in the office looking alert after five hours flying. Fenton was the more gritty-eyed of the two: the QC had demonstrated a good deal of stamina as well as a considerable capacity for the Garrick's brandy.

'He is our man, isn't he?'

Barlow nodded his agreement. The one photograph was a holiday setting in informal clothes, the other a formal dinner-jacketed scene. But the resemblance was unmistakable. The unofficial press photographer had managed to provide a range of angles and one was a very close match indeed.

Barlow looked up at Fenton. 'I'm out of my depth on this one.'

Fenton gave him a rather weak smile. 'If it's any consolation, my dear Charles, so am I.'

He prodded the photographs with a finger. 'I am also, I don't mind admitting, feeling very nervous. I have an

unworthy hope that if I stop looking at those photographs for a moment, they will go away.'

Barlow raised an eyebrow. In the years they had worked together he had never seen Fenton look so unhappy. He had a vision of the network of influence, protocol, and power, that connected Fenton to the man whose picture lay on the desk. Then he pushed the thought aside. Instead he decided on a little deliberate provocation.

'Are you suggesting that we forget about it?'

The question jolted Fenton out of his preoccupation. He was about to rise like a trout to the fly when he caught the glint in Barlow's expression. Instead, he sat up and straightened the photographs until they lay impeccably parallel.

'Alright, Charles, let us put it into words. Our mysterious man, on whose behalf someone appears to have committed murder, is . . .'

Despite his resolution, his voice hesitated for a second. Barlow filled in for him: 'One of Her Majesty's Judges.'

Fenton winced slightly.

'A judge of the Queen's Bench. His Honour Sir Christopher Wilkinson.'

There was a silence. Fenton broke it. 'And now we have somehow to discover just why one of Her Majesty's judges has been hob-nobbing with one of the most powerful criminal figures in the land.'

'No.'

Fenton looked startled. 'I beg your pardon, Charles? Are you suggesting that that man isn't Wilkinson?'

'No, I'm not.'

Fenton wished his headache would go away. 'Then why the emphatic negative?'

'Right man. Wrong question.'

'What do you consider the right question?'

F

Barlow reached across and picked up the photograph with the cut-out heads: 'Why is a photograph of a judge of the Queen's Bench having a drink with a senior criminal so important that a man is killed for possessing it?'

Fenton nodded. 'I take your point.' His face brightened. 'I suppose it is not possible that we are all embarking on a wild goose chase? After all, this could be a purely coincidental meeting of two men on holiday, neither of them knowing who the other was.'

Barlow had not realised before just how deeply worried Fenton was. He had never known him grasp at straws before. His more usual technique was to flick them from other people's fingers. He shook his head.

'I don't think so. If it had been totally innocent they – whoever they are – wouldn't have acted so quickly to stop that poor fool trying to make money out of it. And he was asking, for him, a great deal of money. He knew something – and there was something to know.'

'So, Charles,' Fenton had recovered his equilibrium, 'we are faced with attempting to discover just what that "something" is.'

Barlow got to his feet. 'That's my job, sir.'

Fenton motioned him to sit down again. 'With respect, I am not sure that it is. We cannot go around asking questions about one of Her Majesty's judges. Particularly in circumstances where we have no real evidence. I think this is a matter for the Lord Chancellor's office – a few discreet inquiries through the unofficial channels they have available to them.'

There was a long silence. Barlow's stare was powerful enough to push Fenton backwards out of his chair. It did not. In fact, it was Barlow who was forced to break the deadlock.

'Are you instructing me to forget about this?'

This time the question was real. So was the answer ... one flat monosyllable.

'Yes.'

Barlow planted two large fists on Fenton's desk and leant heavily over them. 'I forget about it. Some lawyer sitting in an office makes a few scribbles on a piece of paper, then he forgets about it. Then we all forget about it.'

Fenton's voice was icy. 'You will apologise for that remark, Charles.'

'I'll apologise for nothing.'

'In that case you will have the goodness to leave my office.'

'I'll do more than that. I'll leave this building.'

'If that remark is intended as a threat, then I shall treat it with the contempt it deserves.'

'That, sir, is your privilege.'

Barlow got to his feet and marched steadily towards the door. He had his hand on the knob when Fenton's voice reached him. 'Come and sit down, Charles.'

Barlow did not hesitate. The door opened and he was half way through when Fenton spoke again – this time in an extremely loud bellow. 'Charlie Barlow! Shut that bloody door and sit down.'

It was sheer astonishment that brought Barlow back into the room. Only once before had he heard Fenton swear and he had certainly never heard him shout. The combination was shattering. He came back towards the desk. Fenton was on his feet, marching towards his private cupboard. He wrenched it open and took out the bottle of malt whisky that lurked in its darkest corner. Without a word he poured a glass for Barlow and for himself. They were large glasses. As he handed one over he caught sight of Barlow's face and began to laugh. Despite his fury, Barlow felt himself grinning back. Fenton raised his glass.

'Your health, Charles. I apologise. I am, as you may have gathered, a trifle concerned about all this.'

Barlow raised his glass in some relief. At least they were back in the world of under-secretaries and understatements again. Fenton leant forward. 'Look at it from my point of view. You are a very senior policeman. Everything you do, every question you ask, by definition implies concern with serious crime. All we have in this case is a photograph. What would happen if you showed that photograph to Mr Justice Wilkinson and told him who Meadows was?'

Fenton raised his hands in mock horror ... 'My dear chap, how unfortunate. He asked if he could share my table ... seemed a very pleasant fellow. We chatted about the weather and how pleasant we both found Cyprus at this time of year. Then I left him ... never saw him again. What did you say his name was?'

Fenton finished his dramatic rendering. Then his face grew harder. 'That would be one version. But just suppose Mr Justice Wilkinson chooses to play it another way' ... Fenton picked up an imaginary phone ... 'Lord Chancellor, I have to draw your attention to a matter of some gravity. I have been cross-examined by a policeman, and a very senior policeman, about some casual event that occurred while I was abroad on holiday ... Naturally, you can accept my assurance that the encounter was totally innocent. But I am concerned as to who authorises this kind of inquiry on such a trivial basis. Are the police getting above themselves? I thought it imperative to bring the matter to your attention.'

Fenton put his phone down but his eyes did not leave Barlow's face. Barlow returned the gaze steadily. He was trying to curb his still-simmering anger and barely succeeding. When he spoke it was very stiffly indeed. 'I would conduct an

inquiry of this kind with rather more discretion than you seem to think me capable of.'

Fenton brushed his words aside. 'You mistake my point, Charles. Let us assume you make your inquiries with all the tact and discretion in the world. But legal circles are notoriously close and quick to pick up the slightest hint of anything that concerns them. What if word were to reach Mr Justice Wilkinson that a very senior policeman from the Home Office had been making inquiries about him without reference to him at all . . .'

Barlow picked up his glass. He only spoke one word but he gave it a wealth of expression . . . 'Lawyers!'

'Alright, Charles,' said Fenton with the air of a man telling an Alsatian to sit. 'You do not like lawyers. I cannot say that I am all that fond of them as a breed myself. But they are powerful and, by definition, they are entitled to regard themselves as being in a privileged position.'

Barlow shook his head very slowly and grimly. 'Not in my book they aren't.'

'We are not talking about your book, Charles.'

'Yes we are. You seem to be forgetting one small fact, sir . . . A murder has been committed – apparently because of the identity of the man in that photograph.'

'But he's a judge!'

The exclamation was wrenched from Fenton. Barlow slammed a fist on the desk. The whisky bottle jumped and Fenton grabbed for it – an expression of anguish on his face. Barlow leant over the desk. 'He's a bent judge.'

Fenton put the bottle back very slowly and looked up at Barlow. When he spoke it was quietly and with careful emphasis. 'You have no proof of that whatsoever.'

'No.'

'What is more, even to suggest that outside this room would be totally unthinkable.'

'Not unthinkable – unacceptable.'

This time it was Barlow who spoke with emphasis. Fenton considered for a moment. Finally he appeared to make up his mind.

'Very well, Charles. You may make your inquiries. But I feel obliged to warn you that, however you may in the past have regarded yourself as a man who lived dangerously, you have never put yourself and your career at such risk before.'

Barlow nodded and got to his feet. But Fenton had not finished. 'I also wish to make one other point perfectly clear. Should your enquiries give rise to any complaint from any official quarter, I shall be unable to offer you any help or protection.'

Barlow grinned at him: 'You mean you'll throw me to the wolves?'

Fenton did not respond to the grin: 'No, Charles. I mean that if it gets to that point the wolves will already be eating me. If they come after you, it will only be with my resignation in their pocket.'

On the strength of that remark, Barlow invited Fenton to lunch the following day. 'We both need some sleep.'

Neither of them had much, but they carefully avoided their major worry until the post-lunch coffee and brandy arrived.

'What do we know about Mr Justice Wilkinson?'

Fenton shrugged: 'Nothing remarkable about him – not as far as his career goes anyway. Standard pattern for the older type of judge ... Harrow, Trinity Hall, Cambridge. Had a good war, as he and his kind would put it. Finished up a brigadier. Took silk. Appointed straight to the Bench. And there he has sat ever since.'

'You pointed out that I don't like lawyers. You're right. I don't. Some of them know too many criminals. Now Wilkinson is a judge. But he was a barrister. I want to know who his clients were then – more particularly whether any of them made a habit of using him for all their cases.'

Fenton's spirits lightened slightly. At least his headache last night had not been acquired in vain. 'I am afraid I have news for you, Charles. Mr Justice Wilkinson never practised as a criminal lawyer. He may have done a few dock briefs when he was starting. But as a silk he worked entirely in the civil courts. His speciality was the law of contract and, even there, he never took any cases which were shady. His stuff was all very dull and very respectable.'

They got up and left, and stood for a moment on the pavement. Eventually Barlow shrugged.

'I know one thing. If Meadows has taken the risk of even making an approach to a Queen's Bench Judge, however gentle and however safe his ground, then one thing is certain. He wants something very big – and he wants it very badly.'

Fenton nodded. 'I know, Charles. If it wasn't for that I would have accepted your resignation.'

A taxi slid past. Fenton threw up a hand, leapt in and was gone. Barlow stood and watched him whirl away. Then he turned and walked slowly in the opposite direction. He looked at his watch. There were two men he wanted to see. One was sitting in an office in Scotland Yard; the other in a cell in Wormwood Scrubs.

As Barlow that evening trudged up the stairs leading to his flat he decided he had been wasting his time. He had managed to drag the man he wanted at the Yard away from his current preoccupation with bombs and terrorists. Indeed, he had escaped fairly willingly into a discussion of conventional crime

with some relief. But he had been unable to offer any useful information about Meadows. . . .

'As far as I know he hasn't got anything big on, Charlie. In fact, if anything he's been very quiet. He's trying to pretend he's just a businessman now – and always has been. I'll tell you one thing, though. He's not fond of you – ever since you took those lads of yours to turn over his nice country house.'

'I'm not fond of *him* either,' said Barlow. 'I thought we had him that time. We didn't. He had hordes of lawyers screaming on his behalf and we had to let him go.'

'But not before you'd given him a rough time.'

'Not so rough. We humiliated him by not treating him as Mr Big.'

'He hasn't forgotten . . . So if you're thinking of going anywhere near Meadows yourself, take someone with you – just to watch your back.'

Barlow had thanked him for the advice and moved on to the Scrubs. His contact there had been willing enough to be distracted, understandably since he was in the middle of the first year of a five-year sentence for robbery. Barlow had not been responsible for inflicting that upon him. He had, however, put Johnny away for two other shorter terms when they had both been operating in the North. His last venture, Barlow knew, had been with a group financed and controlled by Meadows. Reasonably enough, Johnny denied it: 'I've never had anything to do with him personally, Mr Barlow, of course. You know that. But I've heard a lot about him. You're bound to in a place like this.'

Barlow pushed a packet of cigarettes across the table. 'Tell me about him, Johnny.'

'There's not much to tell, Mr, Barlow . . . except for what you know anyway.'

'Anything odd about him?'

'Not really, Mr Barlow. He's a good minder – looks after his boys ... So they tell me, anyway.' Johnny was having trouble keeping up the pretence. 'Keeps an eye on that club of his.'

'What about women?'

Johnny shook his head. 'Not down that end of town, Mr Barlow. Not any more. Mr Meadows doesn't mix much with our lot. If you want to know about that you'd have to ask his posh friends ...'

It had gone on like that for some time. There had only been one passing reference that sounded even remotely interesting. He had been taking Johnny patiently through every single occasion on which he had seen Meadows, and Johnny had mentioned one particular evening when Meadows had paused to talk to someone at a nearby table in the club which he owned ...

'It was funny, that, Mr Barlow. I'd forgotten all about it 'til you started asking me. Meadows was walking past and he suddenly saw this bloke. I think his name was Rogers – that's it, Jim Rogers. Suddenly he leans over, grabs hold of Rogers by the shoulder and says, very soft so I could hardly hear ... "You've been seeing Rosie. I want you to stop" ... And then he walks on again. Except Rogers goes as white as a sheet and starts shaking so much he can hardly get his drink down. Somebody else said something and Rogers threatens to belt him one if he doesn't shut up and, after a bit, Rogers gets up and goes out. That's all.'

Barlow let himself into the flat and picked up the phone. He was undoubtedly on a wild goose chase, but since he had nothing else to do, he might just as well chase wild geese. Or, rather, he would ask somebody else to chase them for him.

The phone was ringing as he arrived in the office the following morning. The voice at the other end was suitably deferential:

'Detective Chief Superintendent Barlow. . . ? Good morning, sir. Inspector Dorsey, West End Central . . . I gather from the Assistant Commissioner's office that you were inquiring about a man called Rogers – Jim Rogers. Did you want to talk to him, sir?'

'Yes I do. Can you bring him in?'

'Oh yes, I think so, sir,' said the voice cheerfully. 'There's usually something we can think of to talk to Rogers about. I'll have a call put out for him and ring you when we've picked him up.'

'Thank you very much, Inspector.'

'Not at all, sir. No trouble.'

Barlow put the phone down. All he could do now was wait.

He did not have to wait long. Four hours later he was sitting across a table from a nervous-looking Rogers in an interview room. The nerves had not been apparent when Rogers had arrived. They had begun to afflict him when the duty sergeant had introduced Barlow into the room, laying heavy stress on every syllable of the 'Detective Chief Superintendent . . .' Now the two of them were sitting in silence while Barlow watched Rogers desperately wondering what he could conceivably have done that merited such high-level attention. Barlow let him wonder. Finally he broke the silence.

'Tell me about Rosie.'

The effect was all he had hoped for. Rogers' face was a mixture of total incredulity and alarm. 'What do you want to know about Rosie for?'

'That's my business,' said Barlow amiably. 'Just tell me about her.'

'You tell me why you want to know.'

'I'm just interested.'

Rogers shook his head. 'Nothing doing.'

'That's a pity.'

Barlow got up and went to the door. He opened it and spoke briefly to the constable outside. Then he returned to his seat and beamed amiably at Rogers. Within a minute the constable knocked and entered. He handed Barlow several sheets of paper. Barlow glanced casually down at them. 'Right.' He pulled his chair nearer to the table and looked up at Rogers. 'This is a list of all the jobs that you could have had a hand in over the last couple of months.' He pulled a pen from his pocket and jotted a few figures down. 'It could come to fourteen years maximum ... depending on how hard I try. Now – tell me about Rosie.'

There was perspiration beginning to break out on Rogers' forehead. But he shook his head stubbornly.

'Alright. Let's talk about the jewellers in Houndsditch instead . . .'

'That wasn't me.'

'So you say. Where were you that night?'

'I was at home.'

'How do you know which night I mean?'

Rogers opened his mouth, then shut it again. Barlow threw the papers down in front of him.

'Don't waste my time, Rogers. I'm busy and if I want to question people I'll pick bigger and better ones than you. I'm not interested in you. I'm not interested in anything you've done. I'm interested in Rosie.'

'I don't know anything about her.'

Barlow leant across the table. 'Yes you do. One night Meadows warned you off her. Why?'

Suddenly, Rogers looked frightened. 'How did you know about that?'

'Never mind. Why?'

Rogers looked wildly around the room. 'How do I know you won't tell Meadows?'

Barlow looked bored. 'Can you think of any reason why I should tell Meadows?'

'I dunno . . .' the voice was barely a mutter. 'Meadows owns a few coppers. How do I know he doesn't own you?'

The room went very still. Barlow leant across the table slowly and with both hands took Rogers by the lapels. Then he pulled steadily until their faces were an inch apart. He spoke in a whisper.

'Listen to me, Rogers. If you ever say anything like that to me again I will personally make sure that you sit in a cell until you rot.'

He pushed hard and Rogers fell back in his chair. Barlow got up, came round the table and stood over him. 'Tell me about Rosie.'

'There's nothing to tell, guv.'

Rogers held up a hand as Barlow made an impatient gesture.

'She's a bird. I fancied her, took her out a couple of times. I didn't know she was anything to do with Meadows. Then one day Meadows tells me to lay off her. I don't know why. But I did. When Meadows tells you like that, you do what he says.'

'There must be more than that. Who is she? What's her connection with Meadows?'

'I don't know, guv.'

'You must know something.'

Rogers straightened up in his chair. 'All I know is that Meadows looks after her. One of the boys told me that he gives her money. But there's nothing there. He doesn't fancy her or anything. She's got a bloke. Irish. His name's O'Donovan.'

'Christian name?'

'Terry.'

'And where do I find him – and Rosie.'

'I dunno . . . I forget.'

'Remember.'

'Somewhere in Clapham . . . Clapham South. By the tube station. And that's all I know. I swear it.'

'Alright.'

Barlow believed him. He turned on his heel and left. He felt like a terrier being sent down one rabbit hole after another. Back in the office he made phone call after phone call: to Criminal Records, to Criminal Intelligence, to stations around south and east London. From each one he got the same answer – no one knew the woman called Rosie. On the other hand, everybody knew Terry O'Donovan. The only problem was trying to disentangle one Terry O'Donovan from another. Barlow was offered an assortment of a dozen ranging from an ex-boxer operating as a strong-arm man to a pickpocket. None of them, however, was immediately associated in anybody's mind with a girl called Rosie.

By six o'clock that evening he was bored and tired and his left ear ached from constant pressure of the telephone. He stared around his empty office and felt a pang of nostalgia for the noise and bustle of his old headquarters – a machine surrounding him with men who knew every corner of their patch and every villain lurking in it. Then, had he wanted information like this, he would have put his head around a door and shouted. Now all he could do was make telephone calls more or less at random into the vast, impersonal mass of London and rely on other people's goodwill and ingenuity to come up with answers.

The door opened and Fenton walked into the office, glancing at his watch as he did so. He looked preoccupied. He also sat down without waiting for an invitation to do so. Barlow braced himself. If Fenton's punctilious courtesy was deserting him, then things were getting very serious.

'I've been listening to gossip, Charles. Gossip about Mr Justice Wilkinson. Only a few scraps here and there. Nothing that amounts to anything ... except that one person who knows him well is rather worried about him. Apparently, he has been very withdrawn recently. The phrase used to me was "as if there was something preying on his mind". The other significant remark was that "it didn't seem as if his holiday had done him much good". As I said, it does not really amount to anything but it is interesting in view of our suspicions.'

Barlow nodded gloomily. 'It may not amount to anything, sir. But compared to what I've come up with it's pure gold.'

'Nothing, Charles?'

Rapidly Barlow told Fenton what little progress he had made. Fenton's face grew longer as he listened. When Barlow finished he was silent for a moment. Then he got to his feet. I must go. I am dining in the Temple this evening ... hopefully I may acquire a little more information there. In view of what you say, however, I think that I may have to pre-empt your inquiries.'

He caught sight of Barlow's expression and held up a hand forestalling any response. 'No, I do not mean that I would ask you to drop the matter. I mean that I regard the possible implications of what we suspect as serious enough to warrant taking the matter out of our hands. I am again contemplating passing the whole thing over to the Lord Chancellor's office.'

'But we don't even have a "whole thing"... just a few scraps of random information!'

'I know. And please do not think I am blaming you, Charles. But the brutal fact is that we have had these few scraps for some time now. We have been unable to add to them. I feel we cannot justify keeping the information to ourselves any longer.

The only thing which would have justified our doing so would have been results.'

'And what will the Lord Chancellor's office do?'

Fenton gave a wry smile : 'I imagine – very little. But at least *we* shall have done all we can.'

Barlow looked as defeated as he felt. Fenton leant across and put a hand on his shoulder.

'Don't blame yourself. No one could have done more. If you would be good enough to come to my office tomorrow morning I would be grateful for your help in drafting my report.'

An hour later, Barlow was still sitting at his desk. Somehow Fenton's consoling words made the prospect of defeat even more bitter. Abruptly, he came to a decision. Action – any action – would be better than sitting staring into space. He reached out and picked up the phone

It was a fairly brief conversation. When it was over the man at the other end scratched his head thoughtfully. Then he pressed a switch on his desk: 'Get me Inspector Jackson, Flying Squad.'

The call came through very rapidly.

'You wanted to speak to me, sir?'

'Yes, Jackson. Have you ever come across Detective Chief Superintendent Barlow – used to be at Thamesford. He's with the Home Office now.'

'No, sir. I know of him, of course.'

'He's just been talking to me – about our friend Mr Meadows. Now you and I happen to know that Mr Meadows is not at all fond of Mr Barlow – with good reason.'

There was an appreciative chuckle from the other end. 'Yes, I heard about that, sir.'

'Right. Now listen carefully, I am about to give some instructions. I want them followed to the letter.'

The instructions were detailed, and when they had been understood – and repeated – the inspector asked a question: 'Does Mr Barlow know about this, sir?'

'No, inspector, he does not.'

'He won't be very pleased, sir.'

'I don't care about that. Charlie Barlow may not know what's good for him. I do.'

The phone was put down and a thoughtful inspector went off to consult his colleagues in the Heavy Mob. It looked like being a lively night.

The club was half empty when Barlow arrived. It was early in the evening for its rather mixed clientele. The knowledge that it was patronised by criminals attracted a steady sprinkling of assorted show business people and politicians who found such association glamorous. But it was usually midnight before they put in an appearance.

Nevertheless there was a quiet hum of conversation. It died into silence as Barlow made his way towards the bar. The barman stared at him with undisguised hostility.

'Scotch,' said Barlow.

He was feeling more cheerful, for he had caught sight of Meadows at a table in the far corner. It looked as if his evening might not be entirely wasted.

Meadows was perhaps a few pounds heavier than when they had last met. Otherwise he had not changed. He still looked like a stockbroker who spent as much time on the golf course as in the City. His face was tanned, and he smiled readily. Only his hands seemed incongruous: they were huge and he flexed them often as though to exercise their separate, restless strength.

Suddenly Barlow stiffened. The door of the Ladies' opened and a young girl emerged and began to walk towards

Meadows' table. She sat down next to him Barlow saw
Meadows lean across and speak to her. He seemed concerned
on her behalf. For no good reason, Barlow felt certain that this
was the mysterious Rosie.

Barlow was watching them in the mirror behind the bar
when he saw Meadows turn in his direction. For a split second
he looked startled and then his face composed itself again. He
spoke to a man at the next table who got up and began to walk
steadily towards Barlow. The man stopped alongside his stool.

'Mr Meadows would like you to join him for a drink.'

'That's very kind of Mr Meadows, but I'm quite happy
here.'

The man put a hand none too gently on Barlow's arm. He
repeated, as if he had learnt it off by heart, 'Mr Meadows
would like you to join him for a drink.'

Barlow looked down at the hand and then up into the man's
face. The man took his hand away. Barlow slid off his stool.
'Well, since Mr Meadows is so insistent . . .'

The invitation might have been insistent but his reception at
the table was hardly cordial. Meadows looked at him with
studied indifference. 'Sit down, Barlow. Tell the waiter what
you want.'

Barlow resisted the temptation to reply in kind. Instead he
took the seat indicated and examined the girl at close quarters.
She was in her late twenties, pretty, dark haired. She also
looked as if she had been crying. Meadows leant across the
table. 'Not seen you here before, Barlow.'

Barlow shook his head. He went on looking at the girl.
When he spoke it was casually: 'Hallo Rosie.'

The astonishment on the girl's face told him he was right.
He had not bargained for Meadows' rage. Taut and white-
faced, Meadows hissed viciously across the table at Barlow:
'Lay off her, copper.'

G

'Dear me, Mr Meadows,' Barlow was beginning to enjoy himself. 'It must be many years since anyone heard you talk like that. I thought you always said "police officer" now.'

Meadows had himself under control now. When he spoke again his accent was back. 'I don't like you, Barlow. I don't like anything about you . . .'

He went on to enumerate various reasons for his dislike. But Barlow was not listening. Instead he was looking at Meadows and at the girl. Their faces were alongside each other opposite him, both at precisely the same angle. And Barlow realised why Meadows was so concerned to exercise his protection for Rosie. He broke in ruthlessly on Meadows' tirade. 'I don't like you either, Meadows. For a start, you haven't any manners. The least a gentleman should do when he invites a stranger to join him is to introduce him – especially to his daughter.'

The guess hit home. The girl's face was a mixture of incredulity and astonishment. Barlow had been aiming at a reaction from Meadows. He got one. Meadows leant across the table and threw his drink straight into Barlow's face.

There was pain as the alcohol smarted in his eyes – and rage. He could feel it as a physical force dragging him to his feet. One hand wiped at his face, the other was pulled back, the one bunching into a fist. But through the fury he heard Meadows' voice mocking at him.

'Come on, Barlow, what are you waiting for?'

That was Meadows' mistake. Barlow tensed himself and fought for control. As his eyes cleared he looked up and saw that four men – big men – had appeared and were standing above him, blocking off the table from the rest of the club. As his brain took command, a chain of thoughts ran through his head . . . Nobody beat up senior policemen, not even in a place like this. The certainty of reprisal was too great. But Meadows hated him for their earlier humiliating encounter. Meadows

owned this club and everyone in it. He, Barlow, was in plain clothes, with no witnesses on his side. It would just be a fight. Started by a stranger who had seemed drunk. Stopped almost as soon as it had started. But not before the stranger had unfortunately been badly damaged. Meadows would apologise profusely. A tragic misunderstanding. If only Mr Barlow had identified himself . . . He might even offer to pay his hospital bills . . .

Barlow took a deep breath and sat down. The four men were still standing over him. Meadows reached across and flipped out Barlow's tie. Barlow gripped the edge of the table. He was in trouble. But his only hope was to stay calm. Whatever happened he could not force his way out of this one. He wiped the whisky from his face while he wondered what else he could do.

It was at that moment that a hand appeared and moved two of the menacing figures aside. A voice spoke deferentially: 'Mr Barlow? Your car is here.'

Barlow looked up. Throughout the earlier encounter, the voices in the rest of the club had continued to keep up a careful level of indifferent talk. Now they were all silent. A uniformed sergeant spoke again, in the same butler-like tones: 'Your car, sir.'

Barlow looked past him. The silence was explained. Just inside the door stood two policemen as still as statues. Alongside them were two dogs panting quietly. Barlow got to his feet and pushed the table aside. He did not look at Meadows or at anyone else as he walked quickly towards the exit. He did not say a word until he was in a Flying Squad Jaguar parked outside.

'Thanks.'

'Not at all, sir,' said the man sitting alongside the driver. 'I'm Detective Inspector Jackson, sir. The guvnor mentioned you

were popping in there and he asked us just to keep an eye on you ... I thought the doggies would make it nice and obvious.'

Barlow squirmed with humiliation. He had had to be rescued like a raw, over-enthusiastic recruit.

'Where to, sir?'

Barlow gave him the address and the unmarked car began to weave its way across London. It was the Inspector who broke the silence: 'What did you think of Rosie, sir?'

Barlow awoke abruptly from his gloom of self-pity. 'You know her?'

The Inspector chuckled. 'Yes, sir. She and I grew up in the same street. Her mum was a very high-stepping lady. Lots of flashy cars used to park outside Rosie's house. She always had more pocket money than the rest of us. She wasn't looking too cheerful tonight, though. I expect she's missing her Terry.'

Barlow cursed to himself. You kept this expensive, elaborate machine. You asked it questions to no avail – and then a man sitting in the car gave you the answers.

'Terry who?'

'Terry Dodge, sir.'

'I got the name wrong.'

'It's the name of her feller. They're married, I think.'

'Where is he then, that she's missing him?'

The Inspector laughed. 'In Wandsworth, sir. On remand. For that platignum job at London Airport. The big one. Him and six others.'

'Are you on duty, Inspector. Or was this trip just a private favour?'

The Inspector hesitated ... 'Well, sir, not exactly ...'

Barlow leant forward. 'In any case pull over at the next pub. I'll buy you a drink and you tell me all about Dodge and the platignum job. All I know is what I read in the papers.'

As it turned out there was not all that much to tell, but what there was proved interesting. The Inspector had been grudgingly complimentary: 'It was a good job, well planned and well carried out. We only caught them because some van driver delivering plastic meals to one of the airlines wasn't looking where he was going and drove straight into them. The other odd thing was that none of them had any real form – not for this kind of job anyway. We don't know who planned it or which of them was the leader. There's nothing pointing to anyone and they won't tell us . . . They won't tell us anything. But somebody is paying for smart lawyers – very smart lawyers. So somebody wants them back in circulation. They may even pull it off too. The three in the van have had it. But the others we only picked up later. They've got expensive alibis. The DPP sat on the papers for weeks before he gave us the green light on all the charges. I reckon there's a fighting chance a couple of them will get off.'

'Including Dodge?'

'Funny you should say that, sir. As a matter of fact, he's the one – sorry – dodgy case among them all. And I've got a feeling he's the brains behind it.'

'What makes you say that?'

The inspector shrugged. 'Just a feeling. He's sharp. He looks experienced. But he's got no form.'

Barlow rubbed his chin thoughtfully. 'A useful fellow for somebody. For who. . . ? Meadows?'

'Could be, sir. We haven't been able to tie Meadows in with this job specifically, though that doesn't mean he isn't behind it somewhere. But I've always thought there was something between Meadows and Rosie, despite their ages. You don't see them together very often, but Meadows always looks keen on

her. And if that's the case, he wouldn't want Dodge out, he'd want him locked up.'

Barlow said nothing. He wanted to talk to Fenton again.

He found him irritably pushing pieces of paper around his desk. He stared gloomily at Barlow and waved him to a seat. 'Good morning. You will be glad to hear that I have discovered the reason for the slight concern being expressed about Mr Justice Wilkinson.'

The irony was very heavy indeed. Barlow sat down and raised an inquiring eyebrow.

'Back-ache.'

'I beg your pardon, sir?'

Fenton straightened a pencil impatiently and repeated: 'Back-ache. The reason, apparently, that our esteemed Queen's Bench judge has been looking worried and not his usual self recently is, quite simply, that he has been suffering from pains in his back.'

Barlow sighed heavily. 'And that's all?'

'That's all. As a result of a dull dinner last night I finally acquired that piece of riveting information.'

'Do we know it's genuine?'

Fenton smiled rather weakly at Barlow's dogged refusal to give up the chase. 'I am afraid so, Charles. In fact, he is coming to London to have treatment for it. That is how my hosts knew. He was due to do big stuff at the Appeal Court in June. He's asked instead to come to town earlier to allow him to receive treatment. And it is taken to mean that his back is bothering him since it is no secret that he thoroughly dislikes sitting at the Old Bailey.'

Very slowly Barlow lifted his head and stared at Fenton. There was such an odd expression on his face that Fenton began to get alarmed.

'Are you alright, Charles?'

'Did you say the Old Bailey, sir?'

'Yes. I told you, if you remember, Wilkinson had little or no criminal practice as a barrister. He has to try criminal cases on his circuit but he prefers the civil courts when he comes to London. But he asked a few days ago to be allowed to sit at the Old Bailey so that he could visit some fellow at Bart's who specialises in slipped discs and that kind of thing ... It is a perfectly reasonable request. Bart's is just down the road from the Bailey.'

'Do senior judges often make this kind of request?'

Fenton thought for a moment. 'I don't really know, but the people I was dining with last night did not seem to see anything unusual in the request, apart from the business of Wilkinson's known preferences ... Why, Charles?'

It had dawned on Fenton that Barlow was still staring fixedly at him with the air of a tiger who had finally caught sight of the goat. Barlow did not reply. Instead he reached out a hand for the telephone and, without a word to Fenton, asked the operator to connect him with the Old Bailey. Once through, he asked a single question. Fenton lost his air of gloomy indifference but he stayed silent as Barlow waited for the answer.

It came, and Barlow, with a word of thanks, put down the phone. 'Did you hear that, sir?'

Fenton shook his head. Barlow thought for a moment and then, assembling his words carefully, told him: 'Mr Justice Wilkinson has chosen to sit at the Old Bailey for the three months commencing on 1st May. On that date the trial will begin of seven men accused of committing a major robbery at London Airport. They are Meadows' men and Meadows, for various reasons, is prepared to go to great lengths to make sure

that at least one of them is acquitted. And he has made sure. He's nobbled the judge.'

It occurred to Barlow that he had never seen Fenton totally at a loss for words before. With a gesture that would have seemed melodramatic had it not been performed so casually, he got up, crossed to the door and opened it. He glanced up and down the corridor, shut the door again and returned to his desk. Then he picked up a pen and looked hard at Barlow. 'Your grounds, Charles.'

Barlow gave him his grounds. He omitted any mention of the meeting with Meadows in the club. That was a personal matter between the two of them. When he had finished Fenton glanced down at his notes. 'Your premise involves a great deal of supposition.'

'I agree, sir. But it fits the facts as we know them. The Inspector from the Heavy Mob couldn't see why Meadows should want Dodge acquitted. What he did not know was that Dodge is not only a key man in Meadows' criminal operations. He is married to a girl who is Meadows' daughter and of whom Meadows is apparently very fond.'

'But, Charles, we are talking about a judge. A Queen's Bench judge. A "red" judge. And you are asking me to believe that this man Meadows has deliberately set out to put pressure on a judge to secure an acquittal.'

'Why not?'

Fenton flapped a hand in irritation. 'It . . . it . . .'

Barlow cut in on him. 'If you are going to say that it has never happened, then let me ask you a question. How do you know it hasn't?'

Fenton was too good a civil servant not to take the point. He nodded grimly. 'Very well. Let me put another point to you, though. Let us assume that Meadows wants this man

acquitted. Why go to the lengths of attempting to influence the judge. Why not just deal in perjured witnesses, false alibis – all the more customary methods of subverting justice?'

'Because he wants to make certain. He has already been informed by his legal advisers that the case against Dodge could go either way. If he rigs witnesses, there is always a chance that the prosecution or the police could bring that into the open. But a clever judge doing a clever summing up . . . moving the jury gently towards "reasonable doubt" in this particular case. And doing it without committing himself to any specific remark that could be pinpointed on appeal. If that happened, Dodge would go free – and nobody could touch him. And the DPP would think even more carefully before allowing charges against him again. Look at the trouble "Nipper" Reed had getting a second go at the Krays.'

Fenton let out a long sigh. Barlow could see him battling against having to accept the truth of what he was saying.

'One more point, Charles. If what you say is true, then Meadows has gone to some trouble in this matter . . . including acting himself.'

'And including issuing instructions for murder.'

Fenton nodded acknowledgement of the reminder. 'Why though, Charles? Just for one man – even allowing for the personal reasons you say are involved. It argues a degree of sentimentality I find unlikely in Mr Meadows.'

'I don't think that's his only reason. I think he wants Dodge out because he has a job for him. A job that only Dodge can do. And that means it must be a very big job indeed.'

Fenton put down his pen and got to his feet. He took the page of notes from his desk and crossed to the wall. Taking his keys he unlocked a cupboard and the small safe inside it. Carefully he placed the notes inside and locked them away. He turned slowly. 'You have done very well, Charles, very well

indeed. The rest you will have to leave to me.'

Barlow continued to stare. 'You fancying yourself as a detective now?'

'I don't follow.'

'Are you going to solve this murder?'

'I have no intention of trying.'

'Then what am I supposed to be leaving to you?'

'Action on this body of – um – speculation, deduction.'

'Action to solve this murder?'

Fenton made a gesture of impatient distaste. 'No, no. I mean action to make sure, somehow, that Mr Justice Wilkinson does not try this particular case.'

'What will you do?'

'I am not yet sure. Some of the law's own delays can perhaps be compounded. This trial brought back, another perhaps pushed forward.'

Barlow was incredulous. 'And that's all?'

'Immediately, I think, yes.'

'And later?'

'Later, with a very great discretion, words can be whispered about Mr Justice Wilkinson, tiny doubts can be cast.'

Barlow sounded contemptuous. 'And Meadows can blow the whole thing up in our faces. You must get it. He has a hold on Wilkinson, a very firm hold. Whatever it is, he'll blow it.'

'And then any whispers from me would not be required.'

'Whew!'

'Don't underrate me, Charles. I simply prefer not to sound too cold-blooded.'

'You *are* cold-blooded enough to keep on forgetting that a man has been killed.'

'Are you so concerned?'

'Totally. No one should be allowed to get away with murder. Not Mr Meadows. Not even a judge.'

'You can't think – '

'I don't know what I think. But I know there's a web here. Meadows is spinning it. That poor picture tout was trapped in it. The judge is caught in it too.'

'Do you plan to rescue him?'

Barlow shrugged. 'Anybody at his level who's corrupt must be past redemption as well as rescue. But he might be persuaded to achieve something in the course of his own downfall.'

Fenton sighed. 'What are your plans?'

Barlow got to his feet. 'Before we can do anything else, we have to find out just what it is that Meadows has on Mr Justice Wilkinson.'

Fenton nodded agreement. 'And the one person we cannot ask is Mr Justice Wilkinson.'

Barlow was moving towards the door. 'I'm not so sure about that.'

'Charles!' Fenton's voice had an extremely sharp edge to it.

'Yes?'

'Be very careful. If Mr Justice Wilkinson is under such pressure that he is prepared to pervert the course of justice in an open court, then breaking the careers of a policeman and a Home Office official will come very easily.'

'I shall be careful.'

Barlow was half way out of the door when Fenton spoke again. 'Charles.'

'Yes, sir?'

'The last time you said that to me six men finished up getting shot.'

Detective Chief Superintendent Barlow sat at his desk staring very thoughtfully at the wall opposite him. The wall in its

Ministry of Works wallpaper stared unhelpfully back. This was not going to be easy. Criminals or suspected criminals were one thing – but how to come anywhere near a man suspected of perverting the cause of justice when that man was himself a Queen's Bench judge?

But somehow it had to be done, and done so carefully that not a whisper should reach his victim's ear. Very deliberately Barlow picked up the phone and began to set some wheels in motion. He booked a phone call to Cyprus for two hours later. A second call went to Scotland Yard to arrange a meeting and to bring from the Yard, within a surprisingly short time, a young detective constable, DC Evans, to a position of attention in front of Barlow's desk. Barlow inspected him carefully: 'You haven't grown any, have you?'

'I've shrunk a bit actually, sir. I had to stretch myself to get into the Force in the first place.'

'Any other changes since we last worked together?'

'I'm a bit older and wiser, sir.'

'Good. We could do with a little wisdom about now. This is what I want you to do.'

DC Evans sat down and listened. 'You just want me to keep an eye on the girl, sir? You don't want me to try and get near her?'

'I most certainly don't. I've cleared it with your people. You report directly to me. And stay away from the Yard. I just want to know everything there is to know about Rosie – where she goes, who she sees, what she does.'

'And you say she is Meadows' daughter, sir?'

Barlow nodded. Young DC Evans looked vaguely unhappy. 'What if Meadows finds out?'

'If that happens, lad, you are in very bad trouble. It will be a toss-up who gets to you first – Meadows or me.'

Barlow nodded dismissal and DC Evans got smartly to his

feet. Before he was out of the door, Barlow spoke once more:
'DC Evans?'

'Yes sir?'

'Be careful, lad. Be very careful. And if anything goes wrong
– anything at all – and you think you may be in trouble, then
get to a phone and ring Inspector Jackson in the Heavy Mob.
Tell him to come and fetch you – and tell him I said so.'

He caught the doubtful expression on Evans' face.

'Never mind about whether it's protocol. Any doubt –
phone Inspector Jackson.'

'Right, sir. Thank you.'

'Don't thank me, lad. You're no use to me with your head
kicked in.'

Evans gave a hollow smile and shut the door behind him.
Barlow sat for a moment staring thoughtfully at the door.
Then he looked at his watch. He was due at the Yard. Stage
Two was about to start.

This time, however, he came face to face with two very
senior colleagues indeed: an Assistant Commissioner and a
Chief Super from the Special Patrol Groups. Barlow told them
what he wanted. When he had finished the AC looked
startled, the Chief Super depressed. The AC recovered first:
'This isn't an ordinary request, Barlow.'

'It isn't an ordinary case, sir.'

He got a snort in reply: 'It isn't a case at all. What do you
think, Donaldson?'

The Chief Super shrugged: 'What I think, sir, is that I have
men on embassy protection duty working round the clock. I
have men looking for Irishmen carrying bombs about. I have
men involved in security precautions all over London. Then
the Serious Crimes lot come and borrow some; any division
with a big football match borrows some more. And now Mr
Barlow wants to borrow some too. In fact, he wants to borrow

a lot. My bucket has got a bottom to it.'

Barlow settled down to argue. This was going to be even harder than he had thought. 'I wouldn't ask unless I thought it was important.'

The Assistant Commissioner half suppressed a groan. 'Of course it is important. Everything that is discussed in this office is important. The question is – how important?'

'It is time somebody did something about Meadows.'

Barlow's remark, delivered in a carefully flat voice, fell on the table between the three of them – and lay there.

'Agreed. You want to do something about Meadows. I want to do something about Meadows. Everybody wants to do something about Meadows. But it isn't that easy. He never puts a foot wrong – not any more anyway. If we had gone after him a few years ago it might have been different . . .'

'We won't go into that now.'

The interruption came from the Assistant Commissioner. The Chief Super acknowledged his error and carried on, poking a finger at Barlow in emphasis . . . 'We can pick up his people when we catch them. And we do. We haven't managed yet to put together a case against Meadows himself – not one that the DPP's office will buy anyway.'

'And you haven't got a case anybody will buy.'

Barlow winced slightly at the brutal statement. 'I know that, sir. But I think my scheme might achieve something.'

'I am entitled to ask for more than that, Barlow. I can't commit men on something as vague as your thoughts.'

This was not going well. Grimly Barlow applied a little muscle – although it was very polite muscle. 'I am sorry to hear you are not able to help, sir. And I'm sure my people will be sorry as well.'

'My people' meant Fenton, as the Commissioner knew perfectly well. His expression remained carefully neutral. But

he and Fenton had clashed before and, as a result of those encounters, Fenton was ahead on points. He wondered if Barlow knew that, then decided that he almost certainly did. He was quite correct. The Chief Super, equally well aware of the fact, decided that perhaps he had better cover his superior officer's retreat.

'Listen, Charlie . . .'

Barlow suppressed a grin. If Christian names were being produced he was as good as home.

'. . . If I could help I would. But you know as well as I do my men are stretched so thin you can practically see through them. Half of them might just as well transfer to the Special Branch for all the use I get out of them.'

Barlow worked up a suitably sympathetic expression. 'I know that. Look. How about this? If I got onto my old lot – up North – and they could spare a few of their people, would you be prepared to let them come in – and brief them. Just for this one job, of course.'

There was a strangled silence while this appalling prospect hovered in the air before the two metropolitan policemen. The Assistant Commissioner found his voice first. 'How long would you want our men, Barlow?'

'A month, sir.'

The AC appeared to plunge himself deep into thought. Barlow suspected he was just counting up to ten.

'Alright. I suggest a compromise, Superintendent. We will provide Mr Barlow with the men he needs for this operation. But not for the period requested.' He turned to Barlow. 'I am afraid that is out of the question. You can have them for a fortnight, Barlow. And that is the best we can do. Is that acceptable?'

Barlow nodded. It was perfectly acceptable. He had doubled up on the time anyway. 'I am very grateful, sir.'

The Chief Super contrived to look even more depressed. But he rose wearily to his feet. 'Come downstairs with me, Charlie, and I'll hand you over to Inspector Jackson. You can brief him yourself.'

The AC rose too and shook hands briskly. 'I'll leave it to you. There shouldn't be any problems . . . I gather Mr Barlow and the Inspector have met before.'

Barlow suppressed the urgent desire to kick him on the shins. Instead, he smiled amicably. 'We have indeed, sir. Thank you very much, sir. Oh, Mr Fenton asked me to give you his regards. He told me to say he was very much looking forward to his next meeting with you.'

The door shut behind them. The Superintendent looked carefully at the wall behind Barlow's ear : 'Fifteen all.'

'What was that?'

'Nothing. Come on. Let's go and find Jackson. Then you can buy me a drink. I deserve it.'

Barlow grinned at him : 'I'd like nothing better. But it will have to wait. I have to go back to the Home Office and take a phone call from another policeman. This one has promised me full co-operation.'

A few minutes later Barlow was sitting opposite Inspector Jackson. A sergeant was there as well, notebook poised for action. Barlow did not want to waste time either. His phone call was booked and he wanted to be back in his office to take it.

'Right. This is what I'm on about.'

He pushed a photograph across the table towards them. It was of the man Turner whose body he and the dogs and Jim Dawson had found in the valley that day that now seemed several years away.

'You'll find the details in the file. I want Meadows'

associates pulled in one by one and questioned about that killing. I want word to reach Meadows from every single one of them that we believe there to be a connection. I want him to get the idea that the connection is established. I want him to get the feeling that he could find himself charged with murder once all the bits and pieces are in.'

Inspector Jackson pulled the photograph towards him and inspected it without emotion. 'It isn't our case, sir.'

'I know that. I'll take care of any problems at that end.'

The Inspector raised an eyebrow at him but was too tactful to inquire just how Barlow intended to explain to one Murder Squad chief that a whole bevy of policemen were tramping around asking questions about his case. Instead he confined himself to more immediate matters: 'How do you want this inquiry conducted, sir?'

Barlow told him: 'I want to give the impression that it is a major operation – as big as Nipper's hatchet job on the Krays. I know it isn't. We have no case for a start. But I want to try and give that impression.'

'And how do you suggest we achieve it, sir?'

'Use as many men as you can. Never use the same one more than twice. Take men off it, put others on. The villains will compare notes. I want them to come face to face with as many different officers as possible. Then they will start asking where this secret squad has its headquarters. The first thing they will think of is somewhere like Tintagel House because that is where Reed set up operations. But however much they ask around they won't find anything – because there is nothing to find.'

'I see, sir. An unprecedented operation being conducted with unprecedented security.'

'Precisely.'

Inspector Jackson looked slightly hesitant. 'Excuse my

H

asking this, sir ... But – why? If there is no case, as you say, why go to all these lengths to invent one?'

'I didn't say there was no case, Inspector. I said we had not got one ... yet.'

'And you think this operation will give you one?'

The Inspector sounded understandably doubtful. Barlow shook his head. 'No I don't. This operation is an elaborate smoke-screen. Something very useful could well come out of it. But its main purpose is to distract Mr Meadows' attention. To worry him and keep him busy watching this apparent threat.'

'And the real threat, sir?'

Barlow got to his feet. 'The real threat will be coming towards Meadows from quite a different direction, Inspector.'

He ignored the inquiring glance and headed for the door. 'Thank you, gentlemen. I'm grateful. Good luck.' The door closed behind him.

'I wonder what this so-called real threat is, sir?' asked the Sergeant.

The Inspector grinned. 'I think that Mr Barlow would answer that question by pointing at his own chest.'

'I heard a story to the effect that Meadows didn't care much for Barlow.'

The Inspector nodded.

'And Barlow doesn't care much for Meadows.'

'He won't get him though.'

'It won't be for want of trying.'

Back in his office, Barlow was taking the overseas call he had booked earlier ... 'Aristide...? You remember the two gentlemen in the photograph? I am sending full details ... No, not in a telex. There is a service flight going out this evening ... with a Ministry of Defence man on board. He is carrying

files. They should be with you first thing tomorrow morning. I want to know everything you can find out about the men. One man is a regular visitor. The other may or may not be. Do what you can ... I'll talk to you again soon. I must go now ... I have to catch a train.'

There was just time. Three hours later he was in Manchester. By a sharp exercise in anti-social bullying he wrenched a taxi away from several people who had been under the impression that they were standing in a queue. It dropped him at the new law courts. As he slid into Number One court, Mr Justice Wilkinson was just delivering sentence.

Barlow sat and listened – and watched. A few seats away another man was watching him. As soon as the disappearance of the duly sentenced prisoner created a diversion, the man slipped out of court and headed for a telephone.

Unaware of the interest his arrival had caused, Barlow continued to inspect Mr Justice Wilkinson. As he did so, he grew more and more depressed. The judge looked tired and ill certainly – in that reports had not lied. But otherwise it was impossible to establish anything of his personality. The robes and wig effectively blotted out the individual who was wearing them. Barlow was fond of reading Trollope. A snatch of dialogue between Lady Glencora, the Duchess of Omnium, and someone or other about getting Phineas Finn acquitted wandered into his head:

'There's no getting hold of a judge, I know.'
'No, Duchess. The judges are stone.'
'Not that they are a bit better than anybody else – only they like to be safe.'
'They do like to be safe.'

Mr Justice Wilkinson looked very safe indeed. Safe and totally unapproachable. But somehow he had to be

approached. The case interrupted so that the judge could deliver sentence on another, now resumed with the man in the dock giving evidence on his own behalf. Barlow listened for a few minutes and decided he did not believe him. The evidence went on. Everyone in court sat watching the exchanges between defendant and counsel. Mr Justice Wilkinson did not take his eyes off the man on trial before him. Barlow did not take his eyes off Mr Justice Wilkinson. The third man, who had slipped back into court, did not take his eyes off Barlow.

The minutes dragged by until, eventually, a door at the side of the judge's bench opened and a grave, frock-coated man slipped unobtrusively in. This was the judge's clerk, and Barlow thought he might provide a line of approach.

Within a quarter of an hour the judge sighed, glanced at the clock, and murmured, 'If this would be a convenient moment... ?' Counsel gave instant and respectful agreement, and the usher called, 'Be upstanding in Court.' He intoned the ritual phrases. '... may depart hence and give their attendance tomorrow at ten o'clock in the forenoon. God Save the Queen.'

The clerk had the judge's door open for him, and Barlow gambled that he would be in the only pub nearby within half an hour.

He was right. Barlow was at the bar when the clerk arrived and contrived to knock over his glass of whisky almost as soon as it was handed him. With many apologies he bought him a large one instead – and they were in conversation. Nearer the door the man who had watched Barlow in court, reported his arrival and followed his departure, smiled at the success of Barlow's ploy.

To get the clerk away from gardening and the weather was not easy but Barlow made some progress. He put on his best musing expression: 'I've often wondered – about judges. They can't behave like other human beings. It's bad enough being a

policeman – always on duty and that. But a judge isn't expected to show any human weaknesses at all. . . .'

The clerk smiled. 'Some judges may find it hard, but not mine. Mr Justice Wilkinson is not a rigid man but I doubt if he has any human weaknesses.'

Barlow signalled the barman across, stifled a half-hearted protest and ordered another round. He threw the question in casually as he paid for the drinks. 'He must enjoy something though. Everyone does . . . even if it's only lying in the sun.'

His companion took his drink. 'I don't think he even cares for that much. He went to Cyprus this year. But he didn't seem very keen. Perhaps once was enough.'

'Been there before, had he?'

The clerk looked mildly surprised at the direct question. Barlow swore at himself under his breath, gently. This man was no fool.

'Yes. Two years ago. I wasn't with him then. He went to recuperate, recover from the death of his wife. She had been ill for some considerable time.'

'I'm interested because I've been to Cyprus a couple of times myself – on business unfortunately. If I had the time and money I'd go back every chance I had.'

The clerk shrugged: 'Well I don't think the judge would concur. I practically had to push him on the plane this time.'

'Perhaps he chose the wrong part. Those beaches down by Famagusta and Limasol are getting a bit like Blackpool.'

'That's the trouble nowadays, isn't it? I went back to Tunis last year and there were hotels and villas all over the place, whereas five years ago you could walk for miles without seeing a soul.'

Barlow saw the conversation heading off down a long predictable road. He decided to take the risk and head it back. His companion was reaching the end of his drink and Barlow

knew he would refuse another. 'Mind you, you have to pick the right time of year for Cyprus. June is the best time. It can get very hot later in the year . . .'

The clerk finished his drink. 'I must go. May I buy you one first?'

Barlow refused as politely as he could, damping his bad temper.

'I'll say goodbye then. Nice to have met you. You should try to convince the judge about the charms of Cyprus. But it was in June that he tried it two years ago – and he didn't stay in the Blackpool-like places. He stayed in Nicosia.'

The clerk gave a cheerful wave and left. In gratitude to the gods Barlow ordered himself a double. He was glancing at his watch and calculating whether Aristide would still be in his office when a large hand gripped his shoulder. A voice spoke softly in his ear: 'I don't like unannounced visitors on my patch!'

Barlow turned on his heel and found an unfriendly Jim Dawson glaring at him.

'Hallo, Jim. Let me buy you a drink.'

Dawson ignored the offer.

'I suppose one of your lads saw me in court. Do you want a drink or don't you?'

'Yes, one of them did. I'll have a large Scotch – and your liver before I'm finished.'

Barlow passed the first half of the order to the barman. When it arrived he took Dawson by the arm and steered him across to a table. 'Sit down and I'll explain.'

'You'd better.'

Two very hard eyes bored into Barlow's.

'I've never liked taking orders – and I'm damned if I'm taking them from you.'

'I haven't given you any orders, Jim.'

'Not directly, no. But my Chief called me in this morning. He gave me deep and mysterious warnings – and I know where they came from.'

Barlow got up, crossed to the bar and returned with two more large whiskies. This was going to be more difficult than he had thought. He stood for a moment at the table with the drinks in his hand. Dawson looked up irritably: 'Either sit down or go away.'

Barlow nodded towards another table, set well back in the corner and out of earshot of any of the other customers. 'Let's move, Jim. Over there. And I'll tell you exactly why I've been poking my nose into what you think is your business.'

Barlow left nothing out – not even his encounter with Meadows. When he had finished, Dawson sat in silence for a moment.

'Alright,' he said. 'I don't like it but I'll live with it . . . on one condition.'

Barlow suppressed a sigh of relief. Life was becoming complicated enough without having a full-scale dispute on his hands. 'What is the condition?'

Dawson stabbed a finger at him in emphasis: 'I've got a murder on my hands. I want the man who did it. If all these fellows from the Met are working for you, then they can work for me as well. I'll lay off, as I said, one one condition. And the condition is that you find out who knocked off that villain and buried his body on the moors.'

He glared at Barlow as he laid the challenge down. Barlow nodded acceptance. He had no alternative even though, as a glance up at the calendar on the wall told him, time was running out.

He was still deep in thought while Dawson sat in silence opposite him, when a voice spoke respectfully and politely above their heads: 'Mind if I join you, gentlemen?'

Barlow looked up and remembered the man who stood there – in his early fifties, neatly dressed with the manner of a not too pompous bank manager. Dawson waved a hand in friendly invitation: 'You remember Harry Brown, the only decent journalist in the whole of the North of England.'

Brown smiled faintly at the claim: he had obviously heard it before. He was an impeccably discreet man with a huge range of sources and contacts who knew they could rely totally on his discretion and therefore told him a great deal that they had no wish to see in the newspapers. Their wishes were always respected. But Barlow also knew that Brown was far more than a mouthpiece. One reason for the respect in which he was held was that no one had succeeded in using him unless it happened to suit his purpose. Barlow mentally flipped a coin. Then he leant forward.

'Mr Brown, what can you tell me about Mr Justice Wilkinson?'

Brown smiled. 'I wondered what you were doing in his court. Wasn't a very interesting case.'

Dawson rose abruptly to his feet. 'I'll get us all a drink.'

It was Barlow's turn to smile. 'Did you tell Jim?'

'Asked him really, Mr Barlow. I thought he'd know what you were after up here. And he didn't.'

'Well now he does. So do you.'

Brown looked thoughtfully at Barlow. 'It would depend very much what you wanted to know about the judge . . . And why.'

'I can't tell you that.'

'Can't or won't, Mr Barlow?'

'Both.'

Brown nodded gently. 'Fair enough. On the assumption that one day you might be in a position to tell me something, I'll tell you all I can.'

It turned out there was not much to tell. Mr Justice Wilkinson lived a life of rigid respectability when on circuit. He dined with the Lord Lieutenant of the county and at a few other houses whose owners were of sufficient status to be acceptable. His judgements were delivered with a total lack of prejudice and personal feeling. He was, Brown thought, a lonely man since his wife's death. He had, however, been afflicted with ill-health in the last few weeks.

Barlow raised an eyebrow at this piece of information. 'You've heard that as well?'

Brown nodded. 'Yes. I am told that he has been having treatment for some back complaint. I don't know where, I'm afraid.'

Barlow contrived not to look too disappointed. It seemed Brown had nothing to offer which could conceivably explain why Mr Justice Wilkinson should be so vulnerable to pressure. He was about to bring the conversation tactfully to a close when Brown spoke again: 'If you want to pursue your inquiries, Mr Barlow, you might try Little Shipton.'

'Where?'

Barlow was baffled and saw no reason to hide the fact.

'Little Shipton.'

'Where's that?'

'I know where it is.'

The interruption came from Jim Dawson. There was an odd note in his voice but Barlow ignored it.

'Why should I try Little Shipton, Mr Brown?'

'Because Mr Justice Wilkinson has a country house there . . . his private retreat.'

'I didn't know that.'

'Not many people do,' said Brown. 'I imagine that is how Mr Justice Wilkinson likes it. After all, the essence of a private retreat is that it should remain private. He's had it about

eighteen months now. I only happen to know because I have friends in the area.'

There was a scraping of chair-legs as Dawson got abruptly to his feet. 'I must be off, Charlie. I'll walk with you as far as the hotel.'

Barlow got to his feet with no suggestion of surprise and they both said their farewells to Brown. They were barely outside the door, when Dawson grabbed Barlow by the arm: 'I'm sorry about that, Charlie. Brown is an old hand, he won't mind.'

'Why the hurry?'

'Because I know where Little Shipton is.'

'You said so.'

'It's only about seven miles away from the valley where we found the body.'

Barlow watched in silence and some sympathy as Dawson unlocked his car. They got in and Barlow waited. 'That's a right turn up for the book.' Dawson sounded rueful.

Barlow was gentle with him. 'You didn't know you had a judge on your patch?'

'Not this judge.'

'Even though he's been in residence over a year??'

'Don't rub it in, sir.'

'Pretty poor lines of communication though. Divisional DI should surely know.'

'I'll take care of him tomorrow.'

Barlow sounded benign. 'How d'you plan to take care of the judge?'

Dawson drew a deep breath. 'I'm going to talk to him.'

'Just like that?'

'Not "just like" anything. I can't talk to a judge as though he were a shoplifter. But I *can* talk to him. I'm investigating a

murder. On that basis I can talk to the Queen of England if I thought she'd done it.'

'The judge didn't do it.'

'You don't know whether he did or not.'

'Neither do you.'

Dawson thumped his fist on the steering wheel. 'I mean to make sure.' He paused. 'Give me one good reason why I shouldn't go and talk to your judge.'

Barlow smiled. 'No reason. It's just ... um ... I'd like to come along.'

Dawson was icy. 'I've passed my driving test.'

'I don't want to drive, Jim, not even from the back seat.'

'Barlow as an observer seems pretty unlikely to me.'

'Agreed.' Barlow remained unreasonable. 'I'll level with you. I want to get near Mr Justice Wilkinson. I want to worry him. I want him frightened if possible. And I want you to do it for me.'

'Why?'

'Because it isn't going to be easy to frighten him. It isn't going to be easy even to worry him with the fragments of nonsense I've got. If I tackle him and it doesn't work, I've had it. But if you jolt him a bit first, then I can get in and have another go.'

Dawson nodded grimly: 'I thought so. Poor bloody infantry, that's me. Expendable. First wave assault troops sixty per cent casualties.'

'Don't play dramatics, Jim. We're the same rank. We're also on the same side.'

Eventually, as he had known he would all along, a disgruntled Jim Dawson drove Barlow up the hedge-lined road that led to the judge's house in Little Shipton. The stiff silence lasted until they stood in front of the door. Perhaps it was the memory of the many times they had been in this situation

before that provided the softening factor, or it may have been the scent of battle in his nostrils. Whatever the cause, as they heard footsteps approaching, Dawson suddenly grinned at Barlow: 'Alright, Charlie. Here we go.'

Barlow grinned back: 'Good hunting, Chief Superintendent.'

The door opened and they both presented serious faces and straight backs. In the doorway, his eyebrows raised in polite inquiry, stood Mr Justice Wilkinson.

They introducd themselves and stated their business. They were shown politely into a study lined with books and invited to sit in comfortable leather armchairs. Chief Superintendent Dawson embarked on his 'routine questions' after an apology for presuming to bother such an important person as a judge. Barlow, who had been presented as plain 'Mr Barlow from the Home Office', sat in his chair and listened. Fairly soon it became obvious that Dawson's routine questions were getting a totally routine response.

The judge had listened to his explanation of their presence with the polite, neutral air that he used on the Bench. He was also showing the same disinclination to join in the proceedings unless forced to do so. However, Dawson pressed on doggedly:

'Were you here yourself that weekend, sir?'

The judge thought for a moment: 'Yes I was.'

'I gather you do a fair amount of walking, sir?'

'As much as I can manage at my age.'

'Did you walk over in that direction at all?'

This time there was no pause for thought. 'No, I haven't walked in that direction for some months.'

'Did you notice any strangers about that weekend, sir?'

'No strangers that I was aware of, Chief Superintendent.'

Dawson sat back and smiled amicably at Mr Justice

Wilkinson. To judge from his expression one would have thought that the answers had been totally satisfactory. There was also a sense that a mundane ritual, necessary but irrelevant, had been completed.

'That is very kind of you, sir. I apologise for having troubled you.'

'Not at all.'

The judge moved fractionally in his chair as if expecting them both to rise to their feet and go. Neither of them moved. Instead, Dawson looked at the shelves of books around him, particularly at a row of paperbacks along his chair.

'You indulge in detective stories, sir – particularly Maigret, I see. I always thought those were very good myself – the best detective on television, I thought. Mind you, real life is not always as well arranged as far as clues go. Take this case, for example. We don't even know why the man was killed in this county, let alone in that particular spot. The only thing we can think of is that he was up here to meet someone. But who would a man like that want to meet up here? If we could find the answer to that question, we would be halfway there.'

He paused as if expecting a response. He did not get one. The judge maintained an air of polite interest but he could as well have been listening to an account of the rain in Spain. Dawson picked up the threads of his gentle monologue apparently unperturbed: 'What was he doing here? Something obviously that was serious enough to get him killed. But he was a small-time criminal – he dealt in petty extortion and blackmail – threatening to make trouble for prostitutes with landlords – that kind of thing. He didn't belong in an area like this ... at least, you wouldn't have thought so. But somebody around here must know why he was here – even if they didn't kill him.'

The judge got rather stiffly to his feet. 'May I offer you both a drink?'

They accepted and the judge turned away from them to pick up a decanter and glasses from the sideboard. Dawson went on talking to his back: 'We did pick up some story about a photograph that he was supposed to have had – a photograph of two men talking together . . .'

His voice trailed away. There was a clink of decanter against glass but when the judge turned round his face was as impassive as before. However, he repeated the word: 'A photograph?'

'Yes,' said Dawson. 'A photograph.' Abruptly he looked at his watch. 'Good Lord. We must move on, sir.' He picked up his drink and swallowed the contents. It did not involve too much effort since the judge's measures were not generous. Barlow did the same. The judge did not press them to stay. Instead he moved towards the door. As they were leaving, however, he spoke to Barlow:

'I am not quite clear what your role is in this operation?'

Barlow followed Dawson out into the hall. 'I tend to have a finger in a good many pies, sir. It is possible that this murder may have some connection with another matter.'

The judge had walked past him into the hall. Dawson had already opened the front door and was standing outside on the step. As if as an afterthought, Barlow took out his wallet. 'My card, sir,' he said, handing one to the judge. 'In case anything should occur to you which might be of interest. Chief Superintendent Dawson is based here in the North. But I am in London – and I understand you will be down there yourself in the near future – at the Old Bailey.'

Mr Justice Wilkinson took the offered card without comment. The three of them exchanged goodnights and the door

was closed. Dawson and Barlow walked to the car and drove off in silence – as far as the village pub.

It was a small cheerful place with a log fire and lots of polished brass and copper. But the two detectives sat hunched gloomily over their drinks. Eventually Dawson pushed his chair back: 'That was a waste of time.'

Barlow prodded a beer mat across the table with his finger. 'What did you make of him?'

Dawson shrugged: 'Polite. Cool. Careful. I can't see any way of reaching him.'

'Too polite,' said Barlow broodingly. 'It didn't fit. If he knew nothing about it and didn't care, he would have been mildly annoyed and ushered us out as soon as he'd answered a few questions. If he'd been interested he would have asked questions and wanted to know details. As it was he did neither. I think he was so concerned with being careful he forgot to be natural.'

Dawson nodded grudging agreement: 'That, yes. But he's no murderer – and no accessory either. I'm sure of that.'

Barlow looked thoughtfully into the fire: 'He may make the connection, though. We've dangled it under his nose. He isn't a stupid man. It may occur to him that, unlikely as it might seem, a man has been killed because of him. Now – if Mr Justice Wilkinson accepts that, what does Mr Justice Wilkinson do about it?'

'Nothing. There is nothing he can do without blowing the whole thing. And having decided to go through with it, he will stick to that decision. He's a man professionally trained to weigh things in the balance. He'll weigh this one.'

It was shrewd thinking and, with growing depression, Barlow recognised it as such. But he pressed ahead with his

speculation: 'There is one other possibility, though. He is a man trained in respect for the law. He has been forced, for some reason – we aren't sure why – to act in a manner which is totally against everything he has ever held sacred. So the pressure on him must have been enormous. If he thought that he was being asked to do even more, to connive at murder, he might swing back.'

Dawson looked sceptical: 'He might. He might not. Either way, there is nothing you can do about it. If he was an ordinary citizen you could pop in and have a chat, twist his arm a bit, offer tea and sympathy – and eventually he'd come the way you wanted. But this is not an ordinary citizen.'

Barlow was still staring into the fire: 'I'm sure I'm right, though. A push and he would come round.'

'But who is going to deliver the push, Charlie? I can't – and you can't. We have no excuse for going back now . . . not just to make conversation anyway. Go back to see Mr Justice Wilkinson and you'll have to go back to make accusations. And you can't do that because you've no evidence. You're stuck, Charlie. Deadend. Stalemate. Stuck.'

Barlow scowled at the flames. He had been fighting not to admit the fact. But he knew that Chief Superintendent Jim Dawson was uncontradictably right.

On the following morning Barlow spent rather less than an hour examining one of the thinnest murder files he had ever seen. The accounts of the discovery of the body were complete enough. So was the pathologist's report. And the murder log of enquiries made was extensive. But there were no leads. 'Not a clue,' said Dawson glumly. 'Not a bloody clue.'

'And none from my stir-up in London either.'

As if in reply there came a telephone call from the Home Office. It was Fenton's secretary reporting that Mr Barlow was

required at Scotland Yard at his earliest convenience. His spirits lifted until she added that Mr Barlow was required not by a working jack but by the AC. 'I'll try for the 10.30,' he said.

'I'll make sure you get it,' said Dawson. 'We've still got a bit of style, and there are still some things I can do around this place.'

Barlow caught his train. In theory it should have left three minutes before he came trundling onto the platform. As it was he was given an impressive salute by an uniformed railway police sergeant standing outside a compartment labelled 'Reserved. Chief of Police'. Barlow was permitted to flop back in his seat before the guard blew his whistle. Sometimes, thought Barlow, it was no bad thing to be a senior policeman.

But in London he was out-ranked. The moment Barlow came into the room he knew he was going to be up against it. Inspector Jackson looked embarrassed; the Assistant Commissioner looked grim. Barlow had hardly settled in his seat when the blow fell.

'I am cancelling the arrangements you requested for surveillance of Meadows and his associates, Chief Superintendent.'

Barlow had expected a fight. He had not expected to be told that he had already lost the battle. He opened his mouth to protest but the Assistant Commissioner forestalled him: 'I appreciate the fact that we undertook to maintain them for a period of time which has not yet elapsed. But I have been making inquiries and I am left with the distinct impression that the men concerned are wasting their time. Time which is very valuable and urgently needed in other areas.'

Barlow struggled to keep his temper. 'I would have thought, sir, that the proper person to assess whether those men are wasting their time is the person who initiated the operation.'

'Except, Barlow, that they are not your men. They are mine.

And I need them. I need them for police work and not for some elaborate exercise in beating bushes. This is a police headquarters, not a grouse moor.'

Inspector Jackson eyed the two men as they glared across the desk at each other. He coughed rather nervously and spoke to Barlow: 'We have been conducting the operation just as you instructed, sir. But in all honesty, we've found nothing, achieved nothing.'

'I'm not interested in achieving anything direct. I am . . .'

It had been a careless remark. Before Barlow had a chance to recover, the Assistant Commissioner ruthlessly interrupted. 'You may not be, Barlow. I am. I am interested in deploying my men to the maximum effect. And I am no longer prepared to allow you to use them as if they were your private army.'

Barlow bit back another angry retort. There was no point. The Assistant Commissioner was the gun but he had a sense that someone else was firing it. He got to his feet. 'In that case, sir, may I express my thanks for the co-operation you were able to extend to me – and my regret that you feel unable to continue to do so. Good afternoon.'

He was practically out of the building before Inspector Jackson caught up with him. Barlow was in no mood for post-mortems. He kept on walking until the Inspector grabbed him by the arm and virtually dragged him to a halt.

'I wanted to say I'm sorry about that, sir. But as you've probably gathered there's been a fair amount of shouting the odds going on.'

Barlow took a step towards the door. 'I'm not particularly interested, Inspector. My operation has been brought to a halt, and that's the only thing that matters to me.'

'Yes, I know, sir. I didn't come to talk about that. But there was a row between the Assistant Commissioners about allocating men in response to an outside request. I suppose it was to

be expected. But there is one thing you should know, sir – though I don't know whether I should be telling you.'

Barlow stopped his walk. 'Yes?'

The Inspector hesitated for a second ... 'I gather, sir, that when a decision was being taken as to whether the operation should continue, there was an inquiry made to the Home Office as to the importance attached to it.'

Barlow knew what was coming. But he prodded the inspector. 'And. . . ?'

'Well, sir, I don't know precisely what was said. But from what I hear – the answer wasn't very favourable to you.'

They avoided each other's eyes. Barlow shrugged himself deeper into his coat, shifted his briefcase into the other hand and headed once again for the door. He was heading back to the Home Office – and there would be a show-down when he got there.

He made straight for the office of Anthony Gordon Fenton, Assistance Secretary. The expression on his face when he pushed the door open was enough to make Fenton's secretary spill her tea. But Mr Fenton was not there. His secretary did not know when he would be there. Mr Fenton, it appeared, was simply not in the building. But when Barlow did eventually storm back into his own office, there was a note on his desk. Mr Fenton requested Mr Barlow's presence in his office at midday on the following day. It was a very formal note.

He sat down at his desk and, squaring his shoulders, forced a grin. 'Confidence, lad. Confidence.' That had been the command of the grizzled Head of CID who first put Barlow in charge of a murder enquiry. Confidence he would show now, despite what he felt.

He telephoned to have a radio call put out for DC Evans: there *might* be something to learn from his surveillance of

Rosie. He booked a call to Cyprus to see if Aristide had any-thing to report. He then began his own report, the one Fenton would expect.

It was gloomy work and Barlow was glad when young Evans appeared. 'What have you got for me, lad?'

It was a sign of the strain Barlow felt that the question was barked at the young detective before the door had closed behind him. He blinked and looked slightly apprehensive. Barlow waved a hand abruptly: 'Sit down. Tell me all about Rosie.'

DC Evans had the air of a man sitting an examination for which he had read the wrong textbooks. 'Well, sir ...' He began hesitantly, then his voice trailed away.

'Get on with it.'

'There isn't much, sir.'

'There must be something.'

It was hard to tell from the voice whether Barlow was incredulous or angry. Evans plunged into his notebook: 'She works in a dress shop in Clapham. She and another girl run it between them. It's a boutique – small, not too fashionable, not too expensive. Does quite well. You know the kind of thing.' He looked up, caught Barlow's eye and went hurriedly on. 'She works there every day. She leaves home every morning. She goes back home every night. She had been out in the evening twice. Once was to the cinema with the other girl in the shop. The other time was for a drink with the couple who live in the flat below. I checked on them – nothing known. Nobody calls on her and she gets no letters apart from the usual collection of gas bills and circulars. The neighbours reckon she is a nice quiet lady – and she is.'

He finished almost defiantly and his notebook closed with a snap. Barlow began to glare at him. Then he dropped the attempt and turned it into a shrug. 'And that's all?'

'That's all there is, sir. She may be Meadows' daughter like you said. But she doesn't keep that kind of company.'

'She hasn't got a feller?'

Evans, being a well-brought-up North Walian, looked slightly startled: 'Her husband's inside, sir – on remand.'

Barlow sighed wearily: 'I know that, son. If I had meant "husband" I would have said "husband". Has she got a feller?'

'No sign of one. The other girl has. She spends half the week at her flat and half the week at her boy friend's. He works in a radio shop in Bayswater. He turns up at the boutique sometimes and he's taken them out for a drink at lunch-time twice. But Rosie always stays on her own. I remained on observation all night for three nights. Nobody came near the place.'

DC Evans abandoned his aggrieved air: 'I'm sorry, sir. But I couldn't see anything that made her any different from a thousand other girls. And I don't think she was just being careful either. Her husband may be a villain but she's straight.'

Barlow got to his feet and came round the desk. He put an amiable arm on Evans' shoulder. 'Alright, lad. It's not your fault. You did everything I asked.'

'Do I give up the surveillance then, sir?'

'Yes you do. You report back to your base. I'm on my own now.'

Evans straightened up. 'You know you've only to lift a little finger to have me come running, sir.' He saw Barlow's embarrassment and turned. 'Good luck, sir.'

Barlow stared as the door closed. 'Getting sentimental in my old age,' he muttered, which could not prevent a warm note creeping into his voice as he talked half an hour later to Aristide. Not that his information was precisely sparkling.

'I have not reported before, Charles, because there is so

little to report.' Meadows – they called him "Green Fields" – had had a lease on a villa in Cyprus for six years. He used it often for brief stays. Aristide was satisfied he had no connection with local villains. 'Perhaps he likes our sun and our wine.'

Barlow grunted. 'And the other one?' Nothing untoward had occurred or least been reported about his stay on the island. He had been a careful tenant of the holiday apartment. The housekeeper had found him quiet, and generous.

'I've found one thing more,' said Barlow. 'He came to Cyprus two years ago. In June. He stayed at an hotel in Nicosia.'

Aristide said a shade wearily, 'We will check. But what do you expect us to find?'

Barlow took a deep breath. 'There has to be scandal. There must be. Something started on his first visit. Something "Green Fields" nailed on him then.'

'There have been not even hints of such a thing.'

This time Barlow snapped his question. 'Not even in the Turkish quarter?'

It seemed as though Aristide was counting a steady ten before he replied in dignified tones, 'There I have not enquired.'

'Then will you, please? And urgently, please?'

Aristide let out a gasp of astonishment. 'For you to say "please" . . .'

'I've a lot at stake.'

The pause was even longer this time. 'I have a colleague in the Turkish police who owes me a favour. He shall pay with this. But if what you call scandal is what he and his religion take as common, accepted, even honourable practice . . . such an encounter, a visit, even several, would cause no comment at all.'

'I think this one may have done. Because I think the gentle-

man in question was appalled at what happened. There may have been recriminations – or, more probably he paid too much money ... Something happened. Something that gave the man a reason for hating himself for returning to the island. Something that caused gossip afterwards, enough gossip to reach our other man in the picture.'

'I follow you, Charles. I will cause enquiries to be made.'

'I am very grateful, Aristide.'

'You are, of course, in a hurry, Charles.'

'Yes.'

Aristide laughed ... 'I have never known when you were not.'

Barlow did not laugh. 'Things have happened since we last spoke to make it even more urgent. Then I thought I wanted to speak to this man about a possible crime in the future. I now think he may have already committed a crime.'

Aristide did not sound impressed. 'Going to bed with boys is a crime in England, Charles. In Cyprus – and in Turkish Cyprus – it is part of the life.'

'I want him for more than that, Aristide.'

There was another silence. Then Aristide spoke: 'I shall be as quick as I can, Charles. If this happened through what we call the usual channels, you shall know within twenty-four hours.'

Barlow felt faintly cheered and turned again to drafting his report. It was nearly dark by the time he finished, and his depression had returned. No amount of careful phrasing could disguise the fact that the report was as gloomy as the street outside. With a grunt of disgust Barlow pushed the pieces of paper aside. It was now definitely time for a drink. He was on his way down the corridor when he heard the phone ringing. He began to turn back and then, with an irritable shrug, kept on going. It was too early for Aristide to have anything to

report: it was probably Fenton delaying their meeting because something more important than Mr Barlow's minor problem was demanding his attention. The phone continued to ring. But Detective Chief Superintendent Barlow turned the corner and left it behind.

He was standing in the entrance hall pondering briefly where to go when he heard the shout behind him:

'Mr Barlow?'

It was the desk porter. He was holding a phone in his hand and beckoning. Barlow resigned himself to the inevitable and walked across.

'They said they'd tried your office but there was no reply, and they were asking me if I'd seen you, sir.'

The porter handed him the phone. Barlow took it and held it to his ear without a word. But it was not the overseas operator who spoke. Instead a more familiar voice said: 'Mr Barlow? I thought I'd missed you.'

It was Inspector Jackson. Barlow wished he had kept on going. He was in no mood for offers of consolatory drinks or further regrets that he had been left high and dry by his colleagues at the Yard.

'Are you there, sir?'

He was suddenly aware that there was an urgency in the Inspector's voice.

'Yes, I'm here.'

'It's about Meadows, sir . . .'

Barlow could feel a faint stir of adrenalin in his veins, 'Yes. What about him?'

'I left the tail on him today. I was going to take it off this evening. It was one of our cabs – I don't know whether you know that we have a couple of taxis we use, sir . . .'

Barlow felt a familiar impatience sweeping over him. 'Inspector, if you are making a report, then make one.'

'Sorry, sir. The tail on Meadows reported at 1600 hours that he left his London flat in what appeared to be a great deal of haste. He got into his car and headed into north London. They followed. They reported at 1700 hours that Meadows was proceeding out of London. He's heading north and he's breaking the speed limit. You didn't tell us much, sir, but I did gather that there was a connection with that killing up there and I thought the information might be of interest to you.'

Barlow took a long, deep breath. 'Thank you very much, Inspector. I'm very grateful. I'm coming straight over.'

He replaced the receiver slowly. He knew he was grinning meaninglessly at the desk porter. The man smiled rather doubtfully back. He was not used to Chief Superintendents behaving like Cheshire cats inside the portals of the Home Office.

'Good news, sir?'

'Yes,' said Barlow. 'Very good indeed.'

He turned away, the porter instantly forgotten. His mind was with a car heading north up a motorway. He was talking to himself as he headed for the door . . . 'Got him. Got him.'

He had to move fast – as fast and as delicately as he knew how.

At the Yard Barlow made a peremptory demand for such modest assistance that it was granted him immediately: the progress of Meadows' car would be monitored throughout. 'Gives these provincial Motorway Patrols something useful to do,' muttered Inspector Jackson.

And Barlow himself could have a Flying Squad Jaguar with a Class One Driver and a multi-frequency radio to go wherever he liked. 'It'll only be a simple journey north,' he said.

He then used priority police lines to call Cyprus. Aristide

was not surprised to hear his voice, though his own had a purr of pride.

'I have it for you, Charles. These things are of no importance here and are soon forgotten, but we were fortunate. Our mutual friend was much distressed by the incident and so it was remembered. It was as you thought. He was noticed during his visit – by a gentleman here who deals in such matters. He escorted our friend around the usual tourist sights and then led him to some slightly more unusual ones. During the course of the evening our friend apparently succumbed to temptation. It was not the only occasion, however. Even though our friend seemed greatly distressed. It was that which assisted the memory.'

'It was a young boy, I take it?'

Aristide sounded surprised: 'But certainly, Charles. There are many such here. It is a part of life.'

Barlow paused. 'And this time, this last April, were there further stories?'

'None. I have double-checked. There you were wrong.'

'Then he must have been *summoned* by Meadows.'

'So it would seem.'

Barlow paused again. 'Aristide! Do you know the name of the boy?'

There was an exclamation of impatience at the other end. 'You want miracles, Charles! No, I do not.

'Can you get the name for me? It is vital I know his name.'

'You want the name of a boy who went to bed with a man two years ago?'

'Yes. If the people you have spoken to remember that much they will remember the boy.'

Aristide sighed heavily. 'It is possible, Charles. I will enquire. I will contact you tomorrow.'

'That will be too late. I need the name tonight.'

This time there was no sigh. Instead Aristide's voice took on an angry rasp. 'You ask too much, my friend.'

'It is very important, Aristide. I would not ask otherwise.' Barlow swallowed his pride. 'It is not just the case, Aristide. It may well be a matter of my career.'

There was silence. The anger vanished from Aristide's voice. Instead, he chuckled: 'Do not worry, Charles. You shall have your name.'

'Can you pass it to the Information Room at the Yard. They will know where I am.'

'It shall be done, Charles. And Charles?'

'Yes?'

'Good luck.'

Barlow put the phone down and breathed a sigh of relief. Then he shrugged as a thought struck him. That favour was going to cost him something! He would be spending the next ten years repaying by checking on every suspect Cypriot in Camden Town. But if he got that name it would be worth it. He looked at his watch. Meadows had been on the road for three hours. He went to the car.

An immaculately dressed young man got out of the driver's seat as Barlow emerged at the main entrance. He opened the front passenger door, saw Barlow installed, and the car began to move. Within half an hour, following a route Barlow had not even known existed, they were crossing the Brent flyover and heading north. The traffic was thinning out but there was still a steady stream of commuters heading homewards. A good proportion of them were driving fast in the outside lane. There was a certain amount of bad feeling and flashing lights as the immaculately dressed young man proceeded to push them ruthlessly out of it.

They had been driving for an hour when their radio crackled. Barlow reached for the receiver. The set addressed

him with crisp politeness. 'I have a message for Detective Chief Superintendent Barlow.'

'Barlow speaking.'

'The message is from Inspector Jackson at the yard. Message reads: "Subject has left motorway at Exit 29 and is heading west. Further communication will be made on Channel 17." Message understood.'

Barlow handed the receiver back. Without being asked, the driver flipped at his radio panel, then reached into a side pocket and passed over a map. Barlow did a few sums in his head. Then he glanced up: 'I want to be two hours behind him. That means we have half an hour to make up.'

The only reply was a hum as the engine revolutions began to build up.

An hour later the radio crackled at them again. This time it was the Information Room at Derby. The voice sounded a trifle puzzled: 'I have a message for Detective Chief Superintendent Barlow.'

'Barlow speaking.'

'It is a message passed to us from the Yard, sir. But it doesn't seem to make much sense.'

'Just read it.'

'Very good, sir. Message reads: "The name is Ahmed. Age fourteen now. Curly hair. A slight limp". Does that mean anything to you, sir?'

'Thank you very much. Message understood.'

Barlow handed the receiver over and sat back gratefully. Aristide had understood!

The driver said: 'We should be at the exit in five minutes, sir.'

Barlow opened his mouth to reply when the radio gave their call-sign again. It was the same operator: 'I have a further

message for Chief Superintendent Barlow. 'Message reads: "Subject has parked in car park of the George Inn, village called Little Shipton. Do you wish further enquiries?" Over.'

'Barlow here. Please pass this message. "No further enquiries. And thank you".'

'Message understood.'

Barlow looked at his watch. There should be just enough time. He unfolded the map and began to give instructions as the driver sent the car knifing across into the inner lane and out along Exit 29.

They were three miles from the village of Little Shipton when the driver braked sharply and pulled in. A car travelling fast passed them going in the opposite direction. They only caught a glimpse of the driver but Barlow felt sure he knew who it was.

'Want his return monitored, sir?'

'Don't think so,' replied Barlow. 'But once he's outside this county it could do no harm to have him booked for speeding.'

'I'll call.' And the driver did, handling the car expertly with one hand.

Five minutes later they pulled up outside the George Inn. An after-hours drinker gave them directions in a slightly slurred voice. The driver was about to move off when Barlow leant forward: 'No. You stay here. Book us in if you can. I'll walk.'

It was only a quarter of a mile and there was a bright moon. His footsteps crunched on gravel as he turned into the drive. There was still a light on in a front room downstairs. The curtains were only half drawn and Barlow could see a figure hunched in an armchair. It was very still. Barlow quickened his step.

There was silence in reply to his sharp ring on the bell. He gave it another hard push and turned away to peer in through the window. But as he did so he heard footsteps slowly approaching. The door opened a few inches and, turning back, Barlow came face to face, for the second time, with Mr Justice Wilkinson.

The judge peered into the darkness. Barlow stepped forward. 'Good evening, sir.'

The puzzled expression on Mr Justice Wilkinson's face was replaced by a look of bewilderment. 'Barlow, isn't it?'

'Yes, sir. I thought you might want to talk to me. Do you mind if I come in?' Barlow stepped past the judge and led the way into the room in which he and Dawson had conducted their first interview. The judge followed obediently and the two of them sat down in silence.

Barlow did not want to start. Everything would depend on the next few minutes. One slip, one false word would ruin everything. He smiled amiably at the judge. 'I gather you had a visit from Mr Meadows this evening?'

Until that moment, Mr Justice Wilkinson had seemed to be in a daze. Now, at Barlow's words, he straightened himself in his chair. With a visible effort, he took control of himself. Barlow saw a spark of anger – simulated or real – in his eyes. 'Have you had the impertinence to put me and my house under observation without informing me?'

'No, sir.' Barlow's voice remained level and impersonal. 'You have not been under observation. Mr Meadows has. Mr Meadows is the kind of man who is frequently under observation.'

'In that case, Mr Barlow, if your concern is with Mr Meadows, I fail to see why you are inconsiderate enough to trouble me at such a late hour.'

'Am I troubling you, sir?'

Barlow got to his feet and moved across to the fireplace. He stood for a moment looking into the flames and then turned to face the judge again. 'Surely, sir, you must see that it is of some interest to the authorities when a figure well known in criminal circles drives a considerable distance to visit one of Her Majesty's judges. I was hoping you might be able to tell me the purpose of Mr Meadows' visit.'

The light was behind him. The judge's face was clearly outlined and he could see a swift flicker of anger, or was it relief? Mr Justice Wilkinson, perhaps because he so badly needed to believe it, thought that Barlow was fishing in the dark.

'My acquaintance with a man called Meadows is extremely slight. I met him briefly during a recent holiday. He expressed an interest in buying my property here. I have been contemplating selling it. He called this evening, explaining that he was in the area anyway on some business matter, to see whether I had come to any firm conclusion. If, as you say, his business activities are suspect, it will obviously influence my attitude towards him considerably. I would prefer, however, to take my own steps to verify the truth of your rather wild statement. And now, if you do not mind, it is late and I must ask you to excuse me.'

The judge got to his feet. Barlow crossed to his chair and sat down. He spoke almost to himself, not looking at the judge. 'Not a wild statement, sir. Meadows is known to have been involved in a vary large number of criminal activities ... or rather the men he employs have been. The latest of their exploits to come to our notice is the airport platignum robbery. The trial is due to take place very shortly.'

He lifted his head and looked straight into the judge's face.

If he had been hoping for a reaction he was not disappointed. What little colour there was drained away. The judge crossed to the door and held it open. 'I must ask you to leave at once. You have been guilty of the most appalling professional misconduct it has ever been my misfortune to encounter. You must be aware that I am due to sit at that particular trial and yet you have commented directly and explicitly upon it. I believe you are in some way attached to the Home Office. I shall inform the Lord Chancellor of this conversation at the first possible opportunity. Doubtless your superiors will then take what action they think fit.'

Barlow made no attempt to get up from his chair. When he spoke it was very softly indeed: 'I don't think you will do that, sir.'

'I most certainly shall.'

'But if you report my remarks to the Lord Chancellor you will have to withdraw from the case yourself . . . won't you?'

There was a long silence. Mr Justice Wilkinson slowly closed the door. He went back to his seat. He and Barlow stared at each other in silence. It was the judge who broke it. 'Mr Barlow, I feel I have been very patient with you. You have refused to leave my house although I have requested you to do so. You seem to feel that we have something further to discuss. I can see no possible benefit in our exchanging one more word. However, if you have anything more to say to me, kindly say it. Then perhaps you will feel able to leave.'

Barlow cursed inwardly. One of his trump cards had been played with no apparent advantage. But at least he was still in the game. He would have given a great deal to know just what Meadows had said to the judge . . . or rather what he had not said. He would have to gamble and make his next move blind. 'I haven't much to say, sir. As I mentioned earlier, I was rather

hoping you might feel able to talk to me.'

Barlow got to his feet again. Deliberately he walked across and stood over the judge. 'Here goes,' he thought. 'All or nothing.'

'Mr Justice Wilkinson,' he said reflectively, talking half to himself . . . 'Of Her Majesty's Queen's Bench Division . . . the product of a good school, a distinguished university, an admirable war record. Mr Justice Wilkinson, may I say something to you. . . ? You make me sick!'

He didn't look to see what effect his words had had. Instead, he pushed on grimly, hitting as hard as he knew how. The Judge sat in the shadow of the chair – not moving.

'You sit on your throne, with the great sword of state hanging behind you, dispensing justice and dealing out punishment to the weak and those fallen by the wayside. And the first time temptation came your way you were far weaker than any man who ever stood before you. Do you know why it took us so long to get near you? Because we knew perfectly well that if we announced that a judge, a Queen's Bench judge, instead of sending a dangerous criminal down for fifteen years, was going to do his damndest to get him off, no one would believe that such a thing could happen . . . A bent judge!'

As he spat the last few words out, Barlow turned on his heel and walked across to the door. He pulled it open, then turned to look at the other man, who still sat like a statue. 'You're quite safe, Mr Justice Wilkinson. I can't make the charge stick. But you are going to have to walk a tight-rope for the rest of your life. Because you should know better than anyone that there is one crime on which the police never close a file – and that's murder.'

The door slammed behind him. He stood in the hall holding his breath with his teeth clenched. Five seconds passed. He

counted them. He had lost. Then a voice called from inside the room . . . 'Stop!'

Barlow counted another five seconds. Then opened the door and came slowly back into the room. The judge had not moved. Barlow stared into the darkness of the chair: 'Yes?'

His voice was harsh. There was no reply and then the judge spoke in an odd, uncertain tone: 'You said "murder"?'

'Yes.'

Barlow reached into his pocket and pulled out a photograph. He threw it across the room. It landed on the arm of the chair and slid to the floor, face upwards at the judge's feet. The judge stared down at it but made no move to pick it up.

'That man. You killed him.'

From the shadow an arm made an involuntary movement as if warding off a blow. Barlow waited – and heard the very last thing he had expected to hear. All the judge asked was, 'How did you know?'

Despite his years of training and experience, Barlow spluttered in consternation, 'You mean you did?'

The laugh he got in reply was chilling. 'Oh no! This is too much. You mean you *didn't* know?'

Barlow steadied himself: 'No, sir. But I have heard what I regard as a confession.'

'Come, come, officer.' The judge was at his most acidly needling. 'A confession is one question? A confession is the words "How did you know?" And a confession made to you alone, with no other witness? It won't do. It simply won't do.'

'Point taken, sir.' Barlow had now fully recovered. 'Mind you, I've heard a lot of confessions, some of them false.' He paused. 'I don't *think* yours was false. But you, better than anyone else, will understand that I need more than your word.

To convince me you need to spell out how you killed him.'

'And why?'

'How is more important. I can make a shrewd guess at why.'

The judge was scornful. 'Policemen's guesses! You didn't even guess that I did kill the wretched man.'

Barlow rasped, 'Tell me how.'

'Is this the way confessions are obtained?'

'People who confess usually want to. Don't you?'

The judge gazed almost wistfully at the fire. 'The time is out of joint.'

'It certainly is when I hear a judge confess to murder.'

'You have it wrong again, officer ... I often seek refuge in bending quotations. I want to say now "You should have come hereafter. There would have been a time for such a word".'

'Hereafter?'

The judge spoke with cold calculation. 'After the platignum trial. I meant to ensure that the man got at least ten years.'

Barlow sat down with a thump, and the judge smiled. 'We have passed the stage of minor protocol, Mr Barlow. Be good enough to pass me some brandy. And help yourself, of course.'

He did, and the judge looked mildly amused at the size of the measures poured. 'You don't do things by halves.'

Barlow took a long slow sip before looking up and saying, very quietly, 'Nor, it seems, sir, do you.'

The judge did not flinch. 'Where shall we begin?'

'In the beginning,' said Barlow. 'I'm afraid I mean with Meadows. Or with Cyprus.'

The judge's face flushed a painful red. 'You know about that – um – that episode?'

'Yes sir. I know when it happened, and where. I know the name of the boy ... Do I have to name him?'

'There is no need. Ahmed.'

'With dark curly hair, and a slight limp.'

There was a sigh from the judge. Barlow said gently in response, 'What I don't understand is why this one episode, why anybody's knowledge of this one episode should affect you so much.'

There was a long pause. The flames danced up as a log dipped in the grate. Barlow could barely see the judge's face which had moved back into the shadow again. He heard his voice faintly from the depths of the chair.

'I was ashamed. All my life I had fought against what I regarded as a weakness, a sickness in my mind. And then in that place, where they seemed to understand . . . I have never forgotten it although I tried to bury the memory of it. And then that man Meadows . . .'

His voice trailed away. Barlow let the silence grow in the room. 'I think I understand. But I think you are wrong. The sin is seduction, corruption of the young. There was no corruption here. And therefore, perhaps, no sin. As you said yourself, they understand – and they accept. I don't share what you call your weakness. But I can understand – and I can accept.'

'I cannot.'

'So you committed murder?'

The judge seemed to recover. 'Exactly.'

'Exactly how?'

'You want to move too quickly, officer.' The judge was back at his near-parody of legal performance.

'In your own time, sir.'

'Would you prefer dictation speed?'

It was Barlow's turn to flush with anger. 'Sir, just tell me.'

'I'd gone to Cyprus to recuperate not from an illness of my own but from the death of my wife who was very dear to me.

She had also, I say this with shame, become a burden. I was both sorry and glad ... I basked in the sun and I found longings in me that were not immortal. I succumbed. And I was again ashamed.

'I came home. I tried to forget. And I succeeded in forgetting the excitement if not the shame. I had returned to my normal, non-emotional, near-frigid way of life when I received, by recorded delivery, just one photograph.'

'Of the boy?'

'Of the boy. There was nothing else. No name. No address ... And my first response was again of excitement, not of guilt.'

'You succumbed to that excitement?'

The judge was immediately judicial again. 'I don't understand the question. You are not helping with these interruptions.'

'Sorry, sir ...'

'Words,' the judge smiled, 'you cannot have uttered since you were a Detective Sergeant. No matter. Let me continue.

'I did nothing about the photograph. And then I got another, again of the boy. This had typed on the back the legend "Ahmed wishes to see the judge again".

'Once more, I did nothing. And I was no longer excited. I was, though, afraid.

'What came next was a telephone call. It was polite, but also peremptory. I was *required* to be in Cyprus – at a time quite convenient for me. I would there, nowhere else, be offered a way out of what my caller described as my dilemma.'

'So you went ...'

'You know I did.' The judge's voice was sharp again. 'I went to lay a ghost.' He chuckled suddenly. 'Odd choice of verb. I mean, of course, put to rest or destroy.'

The judge's voice changed again, and this time his anger struggled with astonishment and disbelief. 'I was, of course, threatened – which I expected. But I was also – what is the phrase – "propositioned" to deny or betray not mere sexual morality but the whole fabric of justice, all that I had devoted my life to.'

Barlow burst out, 'But you consented!'

'You under-rate me, Chief Superintendent.' The judge's voice buzzed with contempt. 'Some things, some standards, I knew I had betrayed. This one I would not. I could not.'

Barlow tried to sound less incredulous than he felt. 'You just played them along?'

'It took ingenuity and manipulative skill. Acting skill almost. I convinced that man Meadows. He is evil.'

'Amen to that,' said Barlow. 'What I don't see is why you didn't come straight to us.'

There was a sardonic look on the judge's face. 'Had I known you I might, only might, have come to you. For the rest – no. Confessing the pressure to which I was subject would have led to my resignation, inevitably. I wanted unto myself the quiet, personal, yes and even the judicial, satisfaction of demonstrating my own probity. After the trial Meadows was welcome to expose me. Not before – not once the very outrageousness of his proposition was clear. This was, as I believe police officers say among themselves, "down to me".'

'Even to the extent of murder?'

'You're too sensitive, Mr Barlow. The man Turner was a worthless creature. He approached me clumsily, without cunning. He had, I believe, but a tenth of the story, as he called it. He had merely a picture of Meadows and myself. I undertook to pay money for it. I arranged to meet him, not here, but at the very spot you found him buried. I shot him

with a .22 Service revolver. The wound was of that calibre?'

'It was,' said Barlow.

The judge sounded cool. 'I had, I think, no real intention of killing him. But I did mean to frighten him. I failed. He laughed. I panicked, I suppose ... Oh, I collected the bullet.'

'None was found at the scene, so that's confirmation too.'

'You shouldn't need it, Mr Barlow. In any case, I can provide more.' The judge moved briskly to a bureau drawer. He unlocked it and produced a file tied neatly with pink ribbon. 'The confession is here, complete.'

Barlow took the file and did not open it. 'He was found buried.'

The judge smiled. 'You will not prove premeditation that way, officer. In that file is a detailed and truthful account of how I left the body hidden as best I could, then returned here for a spade. I buried him the following morning.'

'Phew.'

'Who would have thought the old man had so much guts in him,' murmured the judge. 'The file has a list of exhibits. The revolver and the spade aforementioned, the clothing I wore on that day. The exhibits are under lock and key in a wardrobe in my spare bedroom. Here,' he dug out a key-ring from his pocket and painfully released a key which he handed to Barlow. 'I'd like another brandy now. May I get you one?'

Barlow nodded dumbly.

There was a sudden gaiety in the judge's voice as he handed Barlow his drink. 'What, as the actress enquired of the bishop, happens now?'

Barlow was solemn. 'I think I have to take you into custody.'

'Think, officer? You know you are obliged to.'

'Yes,' said Barlow heavily.

'A waste then,' said the judge lightly. 'Arrangements made. A man killed. All to no purpose.'

'And the waste, sir, of you.'

'You're very generous, Mr Barlow.' The judge took a deep breath. 'You propose to arrest me now?'

Barlow looked at him very hard. 'You do understand, sir, that you cannot be allowed to conduct that trial?'

The judge smiled again. 'Or any trial.'

Barlow snapped back, 'But you can procure one.'

'For myself, of course. I shall make sure it is brief.'

'No, sir. For Meadows. You could do what the police of this country have failed to do – put Meadows where he belongs by testifying against him in open court. You have called him evil. Then put him down.'

The judge was shaken. 'Who would believe the word of a murderer?'

'Who would believe a judge could commit murder except under dire pressure which Meadows in essence brought to bear?'

'I have to say "mea culpa" more than once?'

'It becomes easier with repetition.'

The judge's answer was a swift intake of breath. 'That, clearly, is the way you obtain collaboration as well as confession.'

'By your speaking the truth, sir. No matter who it hurts.'

'This will make,' said the judge, 'a splendid scandal. We must move swiftly then.'

'The Lord Chancellor and the Director of Public Prosecutions are agreed. No time must be lost.' Fenton glanced across the table at Barlow and the Assistant Commissioner from the Yard. Copies of Mr Justice Wilkinson's statements – about the

murder and about Meadows – lay before each of them. 'We must get our hands on Meadows quickly.'

The Assistant Commissioner nodded. 'He's gone back to his place in Cyprus.'

'Has he indeed? Then somebody will have to go and get him, won't they?'

'Yes,' said Barlow. 'Somebody will.'

Aristide met him at the airport with a broad grin on his face. 'You are welcome, sir, to Cyprus.'

Barlow shook hands. 'Where is Meadows?'

Aristide's grin grew even broader. 'By a happy coincidence he is at this moment sitting having a drink at a cafe. You may remember once showing me a picture of it.'

Barlow took him by the arm and turned him towards the car that stood there waiting. 'Let's go.'

As two broad shadows fell across the table, Meadows looked up. His eyes widened as he saw Barlow standing over him. He made a movement as if to get to his feet. Barlow shook his head. Meadows looked past him. Half a dozen policemen were scattered casually around the harbour wall. Aristide took a pace forward and the two of them sat down. Meadows' eyes never left Barlow's face. Finally Barlow leant forward and spoke very softly: 'Finish your drink.'

Meadows did not move. Barlow shrugged. Then he looked at Aristide and nodded. Aristide got to his feet: 'You are John Arthur Meadows?'

Meadows did not even glance at him. His eyes remained fixed on Barlow. Aristide paused and then drew a document from his pocket. He read, formally: 'John Arthur Meadows, you have been declared *persona non grata* in Cyprus.'

Aristide sat down. Barlow drew a notebook from his pocket. But he did not look at it.

'John Arthur Meadows, I arrest you on charges of conspiracy to pervert the course of justice which will be formally put to you on your return to the United Kingdom.'

He closed the notebook and put it back in his pocket. Then he picked up the glass from the table. It was full. Meadows did not move. Slowly Barlow lifted the glass – and drained it.

He watched Meadows being escorted away and called for another bottle of wine. Aristide took only one glass.

'Hail and farewell,' he said gravely. 'I am not a politician, but I have friends in the National Guard.'

Three weeks later Barlow understood. Aristide did not survive the conflict, and Barlow swore never to go to Cyprus again.